Death on ALDER

Beth Everett

First edition September 2015

Cover design by Maggie Olson

Cover illustration © 2015 Edel Rodriguez

ISBN 10: 0692501983
ISBN 13: 9780692501986
Library of Congress Control Number: 2015912891
Beth Fernandez, Portland OR

for Glenn, my true love

I'M TIRED, THOUGHT THE WOMAN, taking off her heavy necklace and depositing it on the dressing table, which was crowded with the cosmetics and sprays she'd applied just a few hours earlier. She freed her hair from its tight bun, and it fell around her face in meager strands. As she removed the mask of youth from her face, her lines and spots appeared again, and she now looked as she felt.

"Not too bad, old girl," she said to her reflection. She tossed the cotton into the wastebasket and rose from her seat, checking the tie on her silk kimono, which had doubled as her gown at the evening's party. The celebration of another year made her keenly aware of the days stacked up behind her, and of how few lay ahead.

While on the short walk from the bathroom and down the hall into the apartment's living room, she could think of nothing and of everything. She looked around the uncluttered space, where the carefully placed relics of her life sat. Things she would "grab in a fire" as she liked to say: an artifact they'd picked up in Panama on their first trip, during the Cold War, when it was thought to be a very bold travel decision; and an early Henry Moore sculpture, two lovers bound, their round limbs disappearing in midair, given to her by a wealthy friend from her New York years.

Absent from the room were any images of her departed spouse. She'd removed them shortly after his death a few years ago. They made her weep, and she didn't want to be the kind of old lady who leaked sentimental tears at the mention of his name. It was her greatest act of discipline, as he was everywhere. She felt him each morning when she made her own coffee, something he'd always done for her, and he was painfully missing as she fell asleep, his soft touch hardest to forget.

It was quiet outside, but the lanterns still shone through the curtains, reminding her of the magical evening that had just whirled by—candles and jazz and finely crafted food and cocktails and the beautiful youth; "her kids," she called them. And yet she'd been so alone at her own celebration. She knew so much that time hadn't shared with them yet. So many of her friends and lovers were now part of history.

But here in this place, with herself as her only companion, there was no loneliness, only the peaceful flow of thoughts, some connected by strands and others streaming without logical connection. She remembered the outdoor market in Paris, her favorite dress with the little rosettes, and how she had met her artist lover. She wondered if she'd ordered enough food tonight, if she'd tipped the caterer enough.

She looked to the space above the fireplace where a painting hung, a painting of a naked woman seemingly stepping toward the artist— her youth in brushstroke. She looked deeply into her own young eyes and released her robe as if to show the woman in the painting her future.

"Nice ta-tas," she said. "Bet you never thought this would happen to them."

Her smooth-skinned years came to mind, her fierce living and the determination to make myths out of the days. Now she was tired, her bones brittle, and her skin soft and loose. She was a wrinkled sage to her neighbors, an old redheaded sibyl, no longer considered wild and reckless.

She heard the click but was deep in the painting now. She could do that, tune in to something so completely that she disappeared. She didn't turn around until the sash from her robe was taken from her hand, and by the time she understood what was happening, she could do nothing about it.

CHAPTER 1

IT WAS ANOTHER DAY OF wind blowing snow into every crevice it could find around my collar and up the cuffs of my jacket where it compressed and burned my skin. I groaned as I pulled groceries from the back of my car. We'd thought it was such a great idea to buy a house with a barn, but having a detached garage in this weather was torture. I pulled as close to the back door as I could. One of the kids opened it, and out rushed our two black labs. The larger and more insubordinate of the two jumped on the paper bags I was carrying, ripping one open. He was disobedient but not stupid, and groceries fell like Pavlovian rewards. He grabbed a block of cheese and bolted while the other dog dashed after him to see if he would share in the bounty. Their black coats gave away their location on the snow-covered lawn.

Many terrible four-letter words were spoken as I picked up a head of cauliflower and several other items from the snow and threw them into the back of the car.

"Can I get some help here?" I yelled.

"I don't have my shoes on," shouted Jack Jr. from the kitchen.

"Goddammit!" I mumbled as I struggled up the icy walk to the door, where I almost fell but held onto the doorknob just in time to save myself. The dogs rushed past me, longing for warmth and looking for the opportunities the kitchen would present to them.

Until I had moved to the East Coast, I didn't know it was possible to freeze and sweat at the same time. I pulled my thick down jacket off and then the wool sweater under it until I peeled down to a long-sleeved T-shirt. I was red-faced. My hair stuck to my head in the shape of a hat, my hands and feet still frozen while I unloaded the groceries in the kitchen.

"Mom! Pepper is throwing up!" my youngest son, Max, yelled from upstairs.

Max was a great kid, but he was not about to clean up dog barf. That was my job. As was carpooling, scheduling doctor's visits, paying the bills, and managing homework, guitar lessons, and breakfasts, lunches, and dinners. My husband was helpful when he was home, but his job in finance kept him at the office until long past dinner on most nights. He was off the hook for household management.

As I headed up the stairs to clean up blue cheese-induced dog vomit, I looked out the window and saw the gusting wind blowing more snow onto my car and porch and driveway.

Living here made me cranky. I was either freezing or wrapped in hot, sticky humidity. During the short months of spring and fall, I'd find myself trying to hold back time like a predator at the door. I'd lean against each day, hoping to slow it down, but instead it seemed to slip around me, one extreme weather day at a time. Add the high pressure of living in the most densely populated state in America to the fact that I had to pay to exhale and that I'd found myself among a population of honking, aggressive foul mouths. An East Coaster would do anything for you—but you'd better hurry up and tell them what you need.

We lived in Forest Glen, a picturesque little hamlet in New Jersey with a commuter train to Manhattan. The residents went to great lengths to create the perfect setting in which to raise their children. A stranger may have thought the town was accidentally charming, but its inhabitants had been historically obsessed about carving out its image. A planning board had to approve the paint color on your house, as well as any structural changes to the exterior. The nice thing about the prohibitive rules was that the town had avoided the rush of new-money monstrosities that had plagued many of the country's suburbs during the real estate boom. The downside was that I wasn't able to paint my house the color I had wanted.

Chain restaurants were banned from our business section, with the exception of a Starbucks, which resided in an old gas station that looked like a small stone castle in a children's amusement park. When the lights were on and the streets were quiet, the town looked like a Thomas Kinkade painting. But sometimes the manicured lawns and seasonally swapped wreaths on the doors made me want to throw mud balls at them. It would have made the cover of the local paper, so I never did.

This perfect facade was infecting my children's sense of reality. It wasn't just the houses that were expected to be impeccable, but our children too. They had college-prep kindergarten where the kids learned pre-engineering concepts and journaling when they were five years old. As they got older, the pressure mounted, and if your child was not keeping up, it could be very difficult on them and us—the parents who had failed them. I was one of those parents. I didn't iron sheets or T-shirts, or make my kids do more than an hour of home-work a day. The school had stopped calling us in for meetings after I accused the last teacher of hating children and suggested she would be better suited for driving little dogs around in the basket of her bicycle during tornados.

I cleaned up the mess the dog had gifted me. As I washed my hands, I looked in the mirror and was reminded that I was growing old in New Jersey. The cold wind had aged my once-perfect skin, and my long dirty-blonde hair was full of winter static. I was still pretty for the mother of two teenagers. I pulled my hair back tight to see what I would look like with a facelift. I'd gained a few pounds from being stuck in the house this winter. I was a walker, and I did my best thinking with my headphones on and my feet moving below me, which was impossible with the weather being what it was. I'd tried, but shuffling down the icy sidewalk like an old person in slippers wasn't my thing.

I thought of pouring a drink, then looked at the time—four o'clock. I never drank before six on a weekday, only on weekends. I mean, who could pass up a couple of Bloody Marys at brunch? And sometimes I drank at lunch with the girls, or a birthday...and on vacation. The rule didn't apply to vacations. But mostly I saved my drinking for after six so my husband wouldn't find me passed out in the hallway when he got home.

Instead, I entered my closet and opened the door to a steep staircase that led to my secret spot in the attic. In the far back corner, my mother's Morris chair, a floor lamp, and an old trunk full of her favorite books served as a private sitting area. I pulled out a small carved box from under a pile of books. It held a half-smoked joint, a small bag of weed, some edible products, and matches. I chose the joint and sat quietly in my little encampment, exhaling more than just smoke as I found some peace in my day.

"Two years," we had said when Jack was offered a job in New York. It had sounded like an adventure then. This was our tenth year living on the East Coast. My kids said "sneaker" instead of "tennis shoe." They played lacrosse instead of basketball. They loved snow days and didn't want to move back to San Francisco because it was now just a place to visit. They had their friends; they loved their neighborhood. This was home now...for them.

The bleak forecast of freezing weather for the next two months made me wish my life away. I wept with homesickness by early

February of each year. My husband would generously tell me to go home even though his difficult life was made more so by my departure. The craving for my sisters and my longing for my city by the bay would overrule any guilt I had about abandoning the family. This year was no exception.

Home meant foggy mornings on the bay and people who said hello when they walked by on the street. It meant restaurants that were open only for breakfast and always had long lines due to their fresh-baked goods and gourmet menus. Home was where you could walk outside every day of the year, where the fleece jacket was the unofficial state garment. Home was a sparkling sunny day, never too hot, when you looked across the blue waters of the bay and saw sailboats, an iconic red bridge, and the soft rolling mountains of the Marin Headlands.

I went down to my desk and booked a ticket to San Francisco with a fourteen-day return date.

There's no place like home.

CHAPTER 2

FLYING MADE ME NERVOUS, SO I took a bite off a pot cookie before heading to the bar. I'd timed the cookie to hit me during takeoff, my most anxiety-filled moment, then I supplemented it with a bourbon and a local stout that tasted like the best chocolate milkshake I'd ever had.

I didn't trust in prayer. I'd broken up with God at age twelve when I found my mother dead from an aneurism. My father had died two years earlier from cancer. I'd prayed then for God to save my father. He killed my mother too.

I put my trust, instead, in things that helped me ease the pain, like bourbon. It had been love ever since I got a whiff of my husband's glass one frigid winter evening. I preferred it to scotch because it was wild like America. Some of my friends saw my bourbon habit as a contradiction to my personality. I'd never used the words "freedom fries" except to make fun of someone who would actually say it. I didn't listen to country music (unless you counted bluegrass). I wouldn't step foot in a Walmart until they paid their workers a living wage. But I loved bourbon. Good old Kentucky bourbon, not Brooklyn hipster bourbon.

I also put my trust in my two older sisters, Lacy and Alice. The three of us were like a long braid, strong and practical but nothing without the other strands. My siblings were away at college when my mother died. Lacy came home and raised me, insisting it would be better for Alice to stay on campus and finish school. She was sister-mother, sacrificing her youth to do the right thing for us. Lacy made sure I got into the best of schools before selling our family home and marrying her longtime boyfriend. My move to the East Coast broke her heart. She thought of my kids as her grandchildren. She had never really forgiven me.

Alice had an affair with a college professor and married him. He provided all the stability she'd lost but none of the passion for life that she needed. As soon as their two kids were grown, she left. A few years ago, she called me from the bed of a bartender she'd gone home with. I had warned her not to *ever* go home with the bartend-er—a rule known to those who were able to live their youth—but she'd laughed and said, "He's different." After two years, which in-cluded a yearlong trip around the world, my sister and Jason, the bartender, were married. They lived in an apartment Jason's boss owned just down the alley from the Jupiter, the bar where they had met. It was the same apartment she'd called me from that first morning while Jason showered, an incredibly funky one-bedroom south of Market Street. I was never sure what Alice loved more, the man or his place.

She was finally able to live the life that she had designed for her-self. She and Jason spent a large portion of their time abroad in Africa, and what she saw there changed her core. Alice returned as a pas-sionate soldier in the war against extreme poverty. She worked for an international organization that fought malaria and tuberculosis. She made her living persuading dot-com millionaires to save their souls through donations. The woman was brilliant and could turn heads as well as any woman in her twenties. I doubted there was a single potential donor who stood a chance against her.

I had self-medicated perfectly, and the first few hours of my flight were spent in harmonious thought. These were times of brilliant thoughts and ideas that, sadly, couldn't be remembered later. The important thing was that I had absolutely no anxiety about flying, and everyone, from the flight attendants to the loud talker behind me, was just lovely—even the guy next to me, who had bad breath and monopolized my armrest.

When my mind cleared a bit, I opened an autobiography of Hemingway I'd found in my mother's trunk. Because of my obsessive nature, I usually read all of an author's works and all the works about them. It was my second time around, as I'd read his books in college. I was different now and so was he. It was like taking a closer look at a respected grandparent and seeing all his imperfections. He used the N-word, disliked Jews, and treated his women like paperbacks, but I couldn't get enough of his adventurous spirit.

Maybe it was the timing, a bad winter, my kids not needing me so much, lack of my own career, or the combination of these things, but I was longing to go on a trip that didn't have an expiration date: Central America or Africa maybe. I would surround myself with trust-fund babies and hangers-on, maybe become a day drinker. I would befriend an interesting local, learn to speak the native tongue without an accent, and make love under a fan in the hot afternoon. I didn't know where my husband was in these thoughts, but he was not under the fan.

Jack. It wasn't that I wasn't attracted to him. I loved his broad shoulders and how he'd kept his rugby-player physique. But his old-money roots could not be shaken. Even when he dressed down, he looked like the kind of guy who'd never had to worry about money a day in his life, and he hadn't. He'd lived every opportunity afforded to a rich white kid. Connecticut equals Connections. I didn't always find this so sexy. He watched my quest to feel less with pity. To me, his sure-footed steps through life had left him incapable of feeling enough. Maybe that made us perfect together.

As we approached the airstrip, I looked out the window and saw the coastal mountain range doing what it did best, holding off the fog that was drifting over its soft crest like a slow wave, fog winning the battle as it always did. The setting sun was dimmed through the thickness of the dense air. Below us, the choppy waters of the bay were dotted with tiny boats and windsurfers. I thought of my parents and then remembered that they were no longer here. Instead, I turned to memories of cold, wet summer days, mist on my face, playing in the sprinklers with a down jacket on, blanket-wrapped nights on the beach, gray days. Gray days. Everything gray. I loved the calm of the fog and still preferred a sweatshirt to a bathing suit on the beach. We hit the ground, and the familiar screech of brakes brought me back.

CHAPTER 3

MY BROTHER-IN-LAW WAS WAITING FOR me at the airport, all Midwestern kindness and smiles. His slender frame and blond hair made him look even younger than he was. Jason had that tan, outdoorsy look that people think of when they think of California, like someone who prefers the bicycle to the car. I felt a little guilty liking him so much. My sister's first husband and I had been very close. I was still getting over the feeling that I was somehow betraying him. Jason didn't break up my sister's marriage though; complacency did. They say money is the number one cause of divorce, but lack of evolution has to be the real cause.

We headed from the deep wet clouds of South San Francisco toward the city. As with every other trip I had taken here in recent years, there was still massive change going on. Industrial shops were now glossy apartment buildings. Graphic designers and high-tech industries were replacing machinist and sheet metal fabrication warehouses in the South of Market area, or SoMa, as it's called. I counted six cranes—indicators of more rising structures in what was once a low-rise city.

"Will it ever stop?" I asked, looking out the window.

Jason just shook his head. "Someone just bought the house down the street for two million cash. Five houses away from a bail bondsman!"

During the late 1990s, there was such an influx of people moving to California that virtually every other warehouse in the area was torn down to provide housing for high-salaried youth. Kids dropped out of college to learn how to program and make the hundred-thousand-plus salaries that afforded them new condos and luxury cars. Companies opened their doors with just a simple idea and a business plan. Twenty-something-aged millionaires brought their dogs to work and rode their scooters around the office. The economic growth was good for San Francisco, I knew that, but I couldn't help resenting the change, maybe because I couldn't be there to take part in it, all of these people calling my city home. Or maybe because these newcomers drove SUVs and parked them on the sidewalk, acting like privileged elite.

We turned onto a tiny alley off the main avenue heading toward the bay. Number Twenty Alder looked like any other low brick warehouse. There was one way in—an antique Indonesian door with intricate carvings and a dark patina, centered on a brick wall. An enclosed alley led to the cobbled center courtyard. Two oak trees had somehow survived wind and time and now created a private oasis. Someone had painstakingly wrapped the branches in tiny white lights, which were blurred by the misty air. Iron tables and chairs and a weathered antique bar graced the worn patio. The courtyard was surrounded by a long, low two-story building on the alley side, with three neighboring warehouses providing the other three walls. Against the back wall sat a tiny earthquake cottage, built quickly to provide shelter to the many homeless after the 1906 earthquake. The lights from the large windows facing it were on in a few of the apartments. The cottage was dark with the exception of one lamp by the window. A wide balcony spanned the length of the two second-floor apartments. Upholstered outdoor lounge chairs lined the open area overlooking the courtyard and the cottage. It was a secret utopia in the middle of a changing urban landscape.

One set of downstairs lights belonged to Martha Byrne, the landlord. Martha's late husband had inherited these buildings in the sixties, and the childless couple had spent all their time and energy renovating them with Martha's eclectic eye. Each unit was unique. My sister and Jason's home had worn wide-plank floors, large salvaged factory windows, and a claw-foot tub on a platform in their bedroom. Not quite the campus Tudor she had lived in during her last marriage.

I saw Martha peek from behind the curtain of her window. She wouldn't invade my sister's privacy by coming to welcome me, although I was sure she knew I was coming. The eccentric landlord was famously good at orchestrating an atmosphere without getting in anyone's way. She had handpicked each and every one of her tenants, and none of them had won their sought-after apartments based on credit scores. You got the feeling you were a guest in a very exclusive club, as eclectic in residents as it was in décor.

In the twilight you could hear the sounds of clanging dishes, low music, and light chatter in the intimate space. *I feel like I'm in an Armistead Maupin tale*, I thought as Jason lifted my bag to carry it upstairs.

"It's supposed to be sunny tomorrow," Jason said.

I sighed. Nothing was more beautiful than a sunny San Francisco day. I couldn't wait to set my eyes on the whiteness of the city and to ramble along the water until I hit the bridge. Someone said the Golden Gate was the only man-made structure that improved on nature. Its strength was perfect in its contrast to the wind-bent cypress and choppy waters.

As soon as the door opened, my sister accosted me like a child squeezing a puppy. I thought my legs would come off the floor. Then she grabbed my face like I was ten years old and said, "Hi, Dummy!" I don't know how it started, but she'd called me that for

years. Sometimes I would answer, "Hi, Dumber," and it would esca-
late from there, usually ending in obscenities and laughter. We did
not have this kind of relationship with our older sister. If you called
her dummy, she would reprimand you and tell you not to call names.
She was a very serious woman. She had to be.

We emptied a bottle of wine while we caught up, but she had to
work the next day, and I was exhausted. I slept fairly well on the pull-
out sofa in the living room, considering the always-present bar that
juts across the center of every sofa bed I have ever encountered. Jason
and Alice were gone when the ringing telephone woke me up.

"Jason left a loaded French press on the counter, and there's water
in the kettle. Just turn it on," said my sister from her office. "I will be
home as early as I can."

"Don't worry about me. I'll be fine. I am sure Lacy is going to
drag my ass all over the place."

"There're caramels in the fridge," she added. My sister had a medicinal marijuana license and always stocked up on edibles when I
was in town.

"Ha! I can manage her for one day. I actually miss her like crazy."

Wrapped in a blanket, I went out to the balcony and snuggled
up on a lounge chair. I sipped my coffee and enjoyed the Cole Porter
song streaming from a downstairs apartment. It was so great to be
outside again. I counted back and figured out that it had been more
than two months since I'd sat outdoors.

The coffee kicked in, and I was ready to move. I folded up the
sleeper sofa and showered in the awkward tub. I imagined Martha
thought this would be romantic—all bubble bath, champagne, and
candles. My sister was at the door before I finished drying my hair.

Lacy was the tallest of us very tall Harding women at five foot
eleven. She used to do some modeling in high school. She was still
gorgeous, even after two kids and decades of marriage. She wore the

big green eyes of our mother and the same full lips all three of us were blessed with, but her face was softer than mine. She didn't fall heir to our father's sharp features. Alice and I had always been jealous of her perfect ringlets. They actually bounced back when you pulled on them. But Lacy had never fully embraced them. Instead, she wore a neat bun, which added to her look of simple elegance.

Her husband was a very successful investment banker. His wealth had given Lacy the freedom to take on a lot of different fundraising causes, including our sister Alice's mission to alleviate diseases of the bottom billion. She'd managed to make life look very easy. Her cars were always new and clean. Her home was magazine-worthy, and her kids were doing what they were supposed to. Lacy was consistently on time and a perpetual planner. She was basically my opposite, loathing my "whatever" attitude about schedules.

After a slightly too long hug, Lacy remembered her plans.

"Hurry up. If we don't get to Ella's before nine o'clock, we won't get a table."

I complied, and we headed down the open staircase to the courtyard. A drop-dead gorgeous man with thick salt-and-pepper hair and a too-tight T-shirt greeted us on the patio.

"Hi, Lacy. I thought I saw your Beamer in the alley."

"Hi, Elliot. You've met my baby sister, Lee?"

We had met before, last year at Alice and Jason's wedding. It was quite an event. Although my memory was clouded with champagne, his was a body not soon forgotten. It was a shame that my husband was more his type than I was, but he was a great guy, and I was genuinely happy to see him again. He had short hair and a chiseled face made perfect by a cleft chin. He always seemed to have a very manly five o'clock shadow. Elliot Trainer could have been a movie star, but he was very queeny, and I wasn't sure he could hide it on screen.

"Of course I remember you. You told me I could borrow that hot little number you wore to the wedding," he joked. "Did you bring it?"

"It's in my suitcase." I laughed.

"We're running out for breakfast," Lacy said as she pulled me along. "Take care, Elliot."

"Enjoy. See you at the party tomorrow night?"

"I can't make it. Previous engagement," Lacy said.

"Oh, too bad," Elliot whined.

"I'll be there," I added, feeling like a consolation prize.

I took notice of his very nice butt as he walked away.

After breakfast, we drove across the Bay Bridge to see my twin nieces, Lacy's girls, who both attended UC Berkeley. They were as together as their mother but a little more capable of walking on the wild side. I was the ever-adventurous aunt, and they loved me almost as much as I adored them. We walked from my nieces' sorority to the colorful Durant Avenue for lunch. Protesters from 1968 were still haunting the streets, only now they were asking for coins instead of social change. Many of the grubby beggars were Vietnam veterans forgotten by their country. Homelessness skyrocketed here after Reagan cut funding for mental health facilities in the 1980s. Warm West Coast cities like Berkeley are a kind place for the country's unwanted. Most of them are from somewhere else, finding the winter nights here easier to stay alive.

After a way-too-short visit, we headed back to San Francisco. It was crisp and sunny, and I loved staring out the window at the new span of the Bay Bridge as it rose up from the depths of the water. I promised myself two years ago that I would be living in San Francisco again before the new span of the bridge reached Treasure Island. It was inching forward, but my family was growing roots on the other side of the country. The torment of having one foot on each coast reminded me of my sad conflict.

By the time we arrived back on Alder, I was melting into the seat with exhaustion. I needed a drink, and Jason was working today. Lacy dropped me off, and I pretended to go back to the apartment, then reversed my path and headed down to the corner bar as soon as she was out of sight. My drinking habits concerned her, and I didn't feel like hearing it. Lacy's idea of a cocktail was a Campari and soda, and she would have just one.

I loved a good dive bar, and the Jupiter was a real find. It was dark and narrow inside, like all good dives. Black booths lined one side, and a simple worn bar stretched out on the other. The walls were cluttered with dingy signs and pennants that had probably been there since opening day. There was no telling why the old place was called the Jupiter. Jason was behind the bar, and I ordered a bourbon and soda after filling him in on my day. He was a great listener and always seemed to be in a good mood. I understood why Alice had to have him. Apparently so did the two girls at the end of the bar. They gave me a jealous glare when he left them to chitchat with me. I felt my claws protrude. I could not imagine how my sister did it night after night.

Wally McCourt came in from the back office and joined Jason behind the bar. His mass of dark curly hair was a disaster, and it appeared he had just woken up. He looked around to see who was in and then headed toward the woman who was alone, which happened to be me. I had met Wally more than a few times by now, but he was such a stupid lush he didn't recognize me. He was Martha's nephew, so I felt like I should play nice, but when he gave me that "hey, baby" look, I could not help but want to mess with him.

"Hey, Wally. It's been a long time," I flirted.

This threw him off completely. I could see his brain flip through his drunken Rolodex.

"Heyyyy..." he replied, squinting, like that was going to help him remember.

"I had a great time last time."

Blank stare.

"Wally, you remember Alice's sister Lee," Jason said.

I laughed. Wally looked relieved and perturbed at the same time. I smiled and finished off what was left in my glass.

"Time for a nap," I said, getting up to head back to the apartment.

"Are you sure you want to nap at five p.m.?" Jason asked.

"Okay, so maybe time for bed." I laughed.

I strolled back to the alley and unlocked the door to the courtyard. The time change and travel were wearing me down, and I was moving slower than usual. When I got to Alice's, I heard voices next door.

"What the hell am I supposed to tell people? You left a mark," said a woman, followed by low sobs from farther in the apartment.

"Let me in! Now!" a man yelled. A banging sound followed.

"You left a mark. I can't believe you did this to me again!" More crying.

I knew the voices to be from Sophie and Myles's apartment. They shared the other second-floor unit.

"Open the door. Now," Myles said with his teeth clenched.

"Leave me alone! You left a mark."

"Open the door!"

More banging on the door followed. I could hear her cries echoing through the common wall. I went into my sister's apartment and slammed the door to make sure Sophie and Myles knew someone had heard them. I was shaking with fear and furious. What to do?

I called my husband. "Hi, honey. You are not going to believe what is going on here. Remember the Princess next door to Alice and Jay's?"

"Oh yeah! Who could forget her?"

Men were so stupid.

"Not funny. She and her boyfriend are fighting. I think he beats her."

"What?" he asked without any of my panic. "How do you know?"

"I heard them! She's locked in the bathroom or something. She's crying and telling him he 'left a mark.'"

"Maybe he gave her a hickey," he joked.

"Hickeys don't make you sob, and the tone is all wrong. Just trust me. What should I do?"

"Stay out of it is what you should do!"

Nothing rattled him, I knew that, but the complacency really pissed me off.

"Oh right. Stay out of it. Okay, I will just let him beat the crap out of her. Or kill her. Maybe he will bury her in the yard like in *Rear Window*."

"Here we go."

"Shut up! You know, you are no good to me here. How are the kids?" I asked quickly.

"Fine. My mom took them to dinner tonight. They're watching a movie."

"I have to call Alice. Talk to you later. Love you, bye."

I dialed my sister immediately.

"Hey, Dummy," she answered.

"Alice! You're not going to believe what I just heard."

I filled her in, expecting her to freak, but she wasn't surprised.

"I was pretty upset the first time I heard them. I confronted Sophie, and she was a complete bitch and told me to mind my own business."

"Unbelievable."

"It's no wonder she wasn't thrilled when I moved in. Well, that, and I threatened her house rule. I finally told Martha a couple of months ago, and of course she was very pissed off. She can't hear it from downstairs and had no idea."

"What about Jason? He's lived next door to them for years," I said.

"Jay is such a guy. He'd heard them before and figured it was none of his business. He also told me it was none of mine."

"Are you fucking kidding me? Jack just told me the same thing. Should I call the police?"

"No, and you really need to move back here soon so you can repair that potty mouth," she said, then continued her story. "Myles left on one of his ship things a few days later. I understood why she's a big fat cheater after that though."

"What? Why stay with him? He's gone half the year, and he beats her."

"I don't know. Maybe he's super hung."

"Eww! He's short, he's never home, and he beats her."

"Who knows? They've been together since she was sixteen. He put her through college, and she gets a lot of freedom when he's gone. Maybe it's a daddy thing."

"He's not that much older than her, is he? Maybe ten years?" I asked.

"Not much older? Do you know how many times you told me Jason was too young for me? Hypocrite!"

I laughed. She was right, total double standard.

"So she cheats on him?" I had to know more.

"Yeah. I know about one guy that she was doing from work. He was coming around for a while when Myles was gone on his last trip. I heard them one night. You can hear things through those walls. It used to be one apartment. They should have insulated better. I guess they've heard us too." She was quiet for a few seconds, and I imagined she was thinking about her own sounds traveling.

"Jason said it wasn't the first time. He wouldn't give me details. He is so *not* a gossip."

"When are you coming home?" I asked.

"Ugh. My director called a six o'clock meeting. I'm sorry, sister."

"It's okay. I'm useless anyway. I'll see you in the morning. We can celebrate my arrival this weekend."

"We have Martha's birthday party tomorrow evening. That should be fun."

I went to the refrigerator and ate a caramel. I called the kids to say goodnight just before the buzz kicked in. Then I wrapped myself in my new favorite blanket and headed down to the deserted courtyard with a drink and *A Moveable Feast*. The calm of the drug washed over me, and I felt every ounce of my soul go edgeless. Nothing could bother me now.

The mix of jet lag, bourbon, and pot left my body a delighted prisoner of the chaise, but my mind was soaring freely. I tried to read but couldn't keep my thoughts on anything but the peace and calm of the courtyard. I noticed that the wall on one side of the property had once had a sign painted on it. It was sandblasted by time, but you could still see the word "mercantile."

The cottage lights were on. Hmm...Dr. Shame Love was in. That was my sister's nickname for the doctor who resided there. The fact that he snuck hookers in and out of the complex was a well-known secret. Alice could see it all (literally once when the blinds were open). I thought Dr. Dan, as everyone else called him, was a little on the weird side, and I never quite figured out why Martha chose him as a tenant. He was shy and vanilla, while everyone else was so colorful. Maybe she found having a doctor there convenient. The residents of Alder loved him though, in a protective kind of way.

I tried to go back to Hemingway, so alive when he recounted those early years in Paris. It seemed to me that the biggest problem he had in those last days of his life was regret. The book was a tribute to his hungry, one-suit beginnings. An empty stomach wasn't so bad when you were doing what you wanted, with the woman that you loved. Yet he threw it away for a step-up with a wealthier, more glamorous woman that he eventually couldn't bear to look at. *Are human beings ever satisfied?* I wondered. The guilt of my own dissatisfaction overwhelmed me for a moment. I really did have it all: gorgeous kids, a loving husband...

I was resolved to find beauty in my own world. My mind went to thoughts of the beautiful oak tree, Grandpa, which stood in our yard, its barren branches highlighted with snow. I wondered where the bunnies went in the cold and imagined them nestled under my shrubs lining the vegetable garden and of of my sweet dogs sleeping by the fire while the kids laughed at the television, my husband watching them with a smile while he read his e-mails on his BlackBerry.

How did they get those lights on those trees? I wondered, my last thought before I fell asleep.

CHAPTER 4

THERE WAS LIFE IN THE courtyard for the first time since I'd arrived. The fog was burning off, but the leaves were still dripping, and the chair seats were wet. Elliot had one leg on a ladder and one on a high tree branch. He yelled, "Hello!" when he saw me on the balcony, wrapped in my blanket, hot coffee in hand. He was hanging lanterns for Martha.

"She'll make me come back up before her party and light them all," he told me.

Each lantern was different. The one he was hanging was rusted and looked like something the military would have issued long ago. Martha had a knack for setting the scene. I knew why she had chosen Elliot for a tenant. It was convenient to have an antique dealer in the house.

"Good morning, Lee!" Martha shouted from below.

She was wearing several long strands of beads and a tunic with more color than I could bear before coffee. Her red hair and glacial eyes reminded me of fire and ice. The sun had never kissed her face, and her smooth, creamy skin hid her age well. I guessed her to be in her late seventies.

"Good morning, Martha. So great to see you again…happy birthday!" I felt like I should thank her for having me, even though she was not my host.

"Thank you, honey. So sorry Alice had to run off. Will she be back soon?"

"Yeah, she'll be back later this afternoon."

"She works too much. Come down to my apartment and join me for a birthday drink this afternoon. Three o'clock."

Never mind what I had planned today—she wasn't asking—but she was such an intriguing personality, and I had never seen her place. I looked forward to it.

Jason was still sleeping, so I threw on my jeans and my favorite New York sweatshirt. With my long, thick hair pulled back into a ponytail, I headed out the door quietly. I left the alley toward Brannan Street and the fog-covered water. As I walked past the Jupiter, all closed up and quiet, I could smell the stale booze from the sidewalk. I thought of all the rummies who must have lost their guts in that place.

Rummies. I laughed. It was a word I'd learned from Hemingway.

A good dive bar was getting harder to come by in San Francisco, and I was happy to know one. When I still lived in town, only real drinkers came to a bar in this neighborhood. San Francisco had a real funkiness then. Here, white kids had dreadlocks, and casual wear ruled. It was a very low-key city, and showing off your money to the general public had never been okay. The environment had always come first here, which was why SUVs had been known to have their windows broken or their tires slashed. But things were changing, and San Francisco's imported dot-com youth had killed off some of the homegrown culture. You could still find it here and there, but compared to what I had known, it was dying fast.

As I walked, I thought about the things on my "must-do" list. My first meal had to be a burrito from the Mission. It was hard to find a good burrito on the East Coast, even in foodie New York City. San Francisco was part of Mexico until 1848. When the armies retreated, they left behind a treasure trove of cultural influ-ences in language, architecture, and food. California was the larg-est producer of agricultural products in the United States. Migrant workers from our neighbor to the south still blessed the state with their gifts, and burritos were my personal favorite. Not some dish of food with sauce covering it. A Mission-style burrito was an enor-mous, foil-wrapped object that you ate with your hands by peeling the wrapper back as you made your way down. No forks needed, and nothing melted or poured over the outside.

On this morning, though, I was on my way to my favorite spot in the city, Aquatic Park. The road met the water and headed toward the Golden Gate. The new waterfront was clean and open. The 1989 earthquake had done the city a great favor when it damaged the free-way off-ramp that ran through this neighborhood. Once the old con-crete structure was removed, a new life emerged as prime waterfront property. A light rail now whispered down a palm-lined avenue, and the exposure to the water and Bay Bridge was breathtaking.

The sun was winning its battle with the fog. I walked past the Ferry Building, thinking of what it used to be. I had preferred it in its old run-down state. Now it was a polished marketplace for locally made cheese, wild mushrooms, and other gourmet items enjoyed by the wealthy. The restaurant where my husband first told me he loved me was located inside. It used to be a little hole-in-the-wall in the Mission District. Now it was chic waterfront—the waiters dressed in head-to-toe black.

I headed past Pier 39 where early rising tourists were already lined up for the boat to Alcatraz. A maintenance guy was hosing down the sidewalk before the daily rush of people overwhelmed the pier. The sea lions were making their usual racket from the docks the city had been forced to give them after they had claimed the spot as their own.

I stopped to watch the fishing boats pulling into the docks on the wharf. The men were unloading their catch for the day. The local restaurants owned most of the boats now, but a similar scene could have been witnessed one hundred years ago. It was said that back then the Italian fishermen would throw what they couldn't sell into a pot, "chipping in" for a seafood stew. And so it was named Cioppino. I thought of all the beefsteak dinners we'd gone to on the East Coast. They were school fundraisers where tomato and steak were served on bread. We had Cioppino dinners in San Francisco—crab and seafood-loaded stew perfected with hot sourdough.

I made it down past the old swim club and into the small cove of Aquatic Park. There were no footprints in the sand yet. The fog was almost gone, and the seagulls were making their usual noise. A lone sea lion was taking laps. *I know*, I thought to him. This was where history met view, the single point in San Francisco that meant everything to me. I used to walk here with my mother. She loved the spot too. It was where I went when I ran away from home when I was seven years old (backpack filled with Top Ramen and my cat). I kissed my first boy here. It was also where I sat and cried after both my parents died. *I know*, I told the sea lion again. *It's perfect here.*

I looked up to Russian Hill, the neighborhood I grew up in. Not a Russian on it, not back then anyway. There were supposed to be some dead Russian fur traders buried somewhere on the hill. I remembered digging for them in our box-sized yard as a kid. Once I found a bone. It turned out to be part of my cat, Truffles. My dad had buried him out there after a car had struck him. They had told me he'd run away. The look my parents had given each other when I showed them the Russian bone was similar to the look Jack gave me when the kids had asked him how Santa got into a house without a fireplace.

On the beach sat a ship-like art deco WPA structure, pure white, like San Francisco itself. The only color came from the tile work on the balcony. The mosaic was unfinished because the socialist artists who were working on it found out that the structure was to house a private club instead of a public space. They walked off the job and never returned, an eternally unfulfilled reminder to us all.

When we were teenagers, we would party up there at night. It was now sparkling with the restoration that new money brought, reminding me of the change that made me feel like a stranger in my own town.

Is sparkling always better? I wondered.

I sat on the beach with my toes in the sand and looked out at the antique ships on the Hyde Street Pier, then past them to the green islands that reached across to the Marin Headlands. The Golden Gate peeked out from the west side, its top still holding onto the morning fog. I was paralyzed by regret. Who knew it would be so hard to come home again?

It was my fault. When I stayed here too long, I sunk into the sadness of my past. My poor husband had no idea of my restlessness when he married me. He knew I'd traveled extensively—I'd lived in Europe, Australia, and Hawaii before I was twenty-three.

Jack swore he would never live on the East Coast again when I'd met him.

"San Francisco is home for my soul," he'd always said.

When I started to collapse into the quicksand of depression after our second son was born, he didn't know what to do.

"Let's go to Europe," I begged. "You can work there, and the kids can learn to speak French." Leaving was so much easier than dealing with the sadness of the memories.

The dot-com bubble burst, and our friends were losing their jobs. Jack was forced to take a position in New York City, and I started to rise again from my pit of darkness.

Now our boys had become East Coasters, and I honked and swore like the rest of them. Our life was fast and busy, and I never had moments like this, on the beach in my sweatshirt, listening to the seagulls yelling, watching the lady with the swim cap do her laps in the cove while the sea lion paid no attention, with home behind me.

I walked onto the corroding Municipal Pier and watched a massive sea lion dip and dive for the fishermen's catch. The water was cleaner than I remembered it. The giant pinniped showed his head, and I shouted greetings to him like I would a dog. He followed me down the pier, hoping for a treat, but he soon figured out I had nothing to offer and abandoned me. I wished I could swim with him. The water was perfectly still at the end of the pier. I spun in a slow circle to catch sight of all that surrounded me: the cityscape, the bridge, the headlands, and the bay. I was high from the familiar beauty.

The bridge called me through wind-blown grass and a long, empty beach. I was starving by the time I got to the small café underneath it and ate a cheese sandwich on sourdough outside on a concrete barrier. I looked onto the rocky breakwater filled with scurrying crabs. The water was wild with confusion, not knowing if it was ocean or bay. I recalled a memory from childhood, a dead black dog floating in the same rocks I looked down at. Home was a whirlpool of comfort and darkness.

CHAPTER 5

I STOPPED BY THE MARKET in the Ferry Building for a bottle of wine and some local cheese and then carried my goods back to the courtyard to meet with Martha. The door was open a crack, so I knocked lightly and sang, "Hello…? Martha…?"

"Come on in, honey. I'll be right out," she said from somewhere in the back of the apartment.

I stepped inside with busy eyes. I had only seen Alice and Jason's apartment and had been curious about Martha's place. The ground-floor home was darker than my sister's. The upstairs balcony overhung the entrance and blocked out the light. Alice's unit was open and modern, while Martha's was vintage in a never-been-renovated kind of way. Knotty pine cabinets and teal laminate counters with a metal trim lined one side of the room. Open shelving on both sides of the living room separated it from the entry foyer. An entire wall was dedicated to overburdened bookshelves, art and design books taking up the majority of the real estate. Over the fireplace hung a portrait of a striking young woman with long red hair. She was standing naked, holding a draped cream fabric of some sort that managed to cover just the right spot. Her long copper hair wound down her shoulders toward her breasts but fell short of covering them. Her creamy skin was almost the color of the muted background so that her hair crackled with heat while the brilliance of her eyes cooled everything down.

"I wish I could have known how beautiful I was," she said from behind me. "We only really learn to like ourselves when the beauty and the youth are gone."

I thought of a photo of myself, in a baby pool with my infant son. When I saw it now, I wondered how my stomach was so flat, but I remembered asking Jack not to take it because of my post-baby weight.

"What was he like?" Alice had told me about the painting, and I couldn't believe it wasn't in a museum somewhere.

"Claude?" she said casually. She was talking about the French master Jean Claude Beaudin as if he had been the local butcher. "Talented, but he smelled like conceit and Bordeaux. He called me Lilith. I met him in the market, and he asked me to model for him. I thought he was a pervert and was going to say no when a girlfriend of mine, a French girl, told me that I couldn't. 'It's a great honor to be painted by Jean Claude,' she'd urged. Well, of course I knew who that was, and suddenly he wasn't nearly as ugly and only half as old."

We shared a laugh. Charles Mingus was spinning inside a console that probably hadn't been moved since the day it arrived.

"I was modeling for him, not for this, but earlier." She pointed toward the painting. "And it was quite innocent, although he was plying me with wine and compliments. It was a brittle day, and there was a gorgeous fire burning in his studio. Suddenly his wife came screeching in like a rabid cat, calling me 'whore Américaine,' throwing my clothing outside in the snowy alley, and swiping at him. She had been his model also, so she knew what was coming, being wife number two. Well, that was it for me! I slept with him that very day. We had a lovely little affair, and then I moved on. I was young and rich, and he was sentimental and brooding."

She motioned me to sit and poured me a glass of wine.

"I'd forgotten all about the painting until he died in 1980. He'd held on to it all of those years and then left it to me. Isn't that wild?"

It was quiet while we rebuilt the glowing embers of that day in our minds.

"How'd you end up in San Francisco?" I asked her.

"I met a poet in New York. Zelda was the first flapper. I was the first groupie." She chuckled. "It was never going to work. I was exactly what he was rebelling against. I was an orphan, like you girls, but with my tragedy came financial freedom."

Alice had told me that Martha was a trust-fund baby. I had also been left with financial security in the ashes of death. My husband was very uncomfortable with it. We never touched the money but instead put it way for the boys. I often wondered if it would be a curse to them later.

"He moved to the Haight when the rents rose in North Beach. I stayed behind once I realized that he thrived on hunger and I was always full. And then I met Harry." Her voice changed now, from eagle to songbird. "It was pure and honest, and we were both ready. He was the truest thing in my life. I know it's cliché, but sometimes the best things are." She took a deep breath and made a physical motion to shake off.

"I'm sorry," I whispered, then said, "This place is incredible. You have an amazing eye, Martha." I stood up now, admiring the objects of beauty and their soft coat of dust. The scent of milestones lingered in the room. "How did you and Harry meet?" I asked, but she wasn't up for talking about that.

"Why don't you tell me how you like living in New York?"

This was the part I always hated. Thanks to the media, living across the Hudson River was embarrassing. When I was growing up, my impression of New Jersey was of girls with feathered roach-clip earrings and Trans Am-driving Bon Jovi lovers. Now there were reality shows about people with names for their abs and animal-print-clad housewives who wasted their lives consuming fluff. There were more malls per square mile in New Jersey than in any other state in the Union. There was another side though. Lush tree canopies, the charming architecture, and the wonderful little neighborhoods...

"When we first moved to the East Coast, we lived in Hoboken, which is on the Hudson," I said.

"Funny, you wouldn't have stepped foot in there back in the day. It was a tough town. Now I hear it's all condos and yuppies."

I smiled. I had heard the stories and seen *On the Waterfront.*

"They were tearing down the old piers and warehouses on the river when we arrived, replacing them with high-rises. It was still a tough place though," I added. "I loved the five-minute train ride to Manhattan, the views of the New York skyline." I could still see the blood-red moon over Manhattan during a historic blackout... "But the kids weren't thriving there. Our son was beat up by a sixteen-year-old kid with six prior assault charges against him, so we fled to the suburbs. I couldn't bear the idea of my kids not being able to walk home from school or play in the park by themselves."

She raised her eyebrows in surprise.

"A city is a city," I said. "We have our share of issues where we live now too. I still feel kind of guilty for running away from it though. I've spent a lot of time thinking about that sixteen-year-old kid. He never stood a chance, a father in prison, five siblings..."

"You did the right thing. You put your family first."

"I guess. It's very pretty where we live now. Tree-lined streets and a charming little downtown, and the schools are wonderful. My husband, Jack, commutes to New York, which is just a hop."

"I've never understood why they make the bottle so damned small." She poured what was left of the wine into our glasses, then walked to the kitchen and retrieved another bottle.

"What do you do, Lee?" she asked.

"Ahh, well, I've been home with the kids since they were born."

"Why do you sound so ashamed of it? What were you before mother?"

"I was working my way up in an investment banking firm when Jack and I met. I would have made VP the year I had Jack Jr. It was impossible for me to leave that little soft baby. They extended my time off and then extended again until they finally asked me to make a decision. I chose my child. I've never loved being home though. The monotony of daily tasks kills me sometimes. The time with my sons has been wonderful though. I don't mean to sound ungrateful; I've loved being a full-time mother to my kids."

"In a way I think it's lucky I never had kids. I've been able to do what I want. But I wonder what was missed. And now, as I grow older, I wonder who will take care of me. It's all going to be on Wally."

"He's a good kid. He really is," she said. Martha had seen my eyebrows tighten, just for that second.

"It's time to dream, kid. What's your dream?"

This was awkward for me because I really didn't know. My practice of motherhood was a blessing and a curse. It had taken from me any sense of personal ambition while leaving me with only a temporary task. Fulfilling as it had been, I knew it was coming to an end.

"I need to figure that out."

"Well, life is about the journey, Lee. Isn't that beautiful? One long adventure full of skips and falls, dances and blunders, spins and staggers. Embrace them! They make up our lives. The only ones we get to have."

"I've been so focused on coming home as an answer..."

"New York City is the center of the universe! You should be enjoying the hell out of it."

"I do! Really. I do. I try to take advantage in every way I can. But the weather kills me, and I miss my sisters…I can hear myself. I'm really using that as an excuse." I chuckled nervously.

"I lived in New York in the days of Sardi's and Toots Shor's. I can't tell you the fun we had. What wild things we were." She wandered into the memories for a moment. "We couldn't get in anywhere without an escort back then." She was looking past me, recalling something.

"Really?"

"You could not get past the door without a man," she said. "Like we were just weak little things without them. I'll tell you what though, we did get around. But it was all hush-hush. No one talked about sex. And if you got knocked up, forget it! You had to marry the bum. You know what our generation was? A bunch of hypocrites and liars… Oh! And alcoholics," she added, laughing while she held her glass of wine up to toast me. "Only we didn't call them that then. You were a drinker, and it wasn't a disease."

"Did you ever see Hemingway at Toots Shor's?" The reference to alcohol reminded me of him.

"That old bastard?" She laughed. "No. But he would pop into the Ritz once in a while when I was in Paris. And we would see him at Gertrude and Alice's house before they had a falling out. He didn't get along with anyone for long. Not even a wife."

I was in awe of her life.

"New York is different now, but Sardi's is still there, thank God. I think the menu might be the same as it was fifty years ago," I added, and we both laughed.

"Lee." She was serious now. "I was your age yesterday, and tomorrow I will be dead. Don't worry about what you are today. Worry about who you want to be and how you're going to get there."

My eyes filled with tears. I was overwhelmed with the emotion I'd been feeling so often lately. The wine didn't help. "I really don't know," I said.

"Figure it out while you can still enjoy it, honey," she said. "Well, enough of my nosing around in your life. I'd better get myself together for tonight."

I felt like I was leaving the cave of some ancient Greek oracle.

CHAPTER 6

THE SMELL OF THE FRESHLY hosed-down patio filled the air. Counting Crows played on a radio, but there was an intimate hush of preparation. Elliot was back up on the ladder, lighting the lanterns he'd hung earlier with long matches. A stranger in a white apron wiped down glasses at the bar. I waved as I walked up the staircase.

It was Jason's day off, and he was in the kitchen when I walked in. "Hey, where have you been, stranger?" he asked.

"Drinking wine at Martha's. She's amazing." I was so groggy it was ridiculous.

"Isn't she? She's getting an early start tonight? Good for her."

There was pretty much nothing anyone could do that would not be okay with Jason. He was always happy and thought everything was great. I couldn't stand this about him at first. I thought he was a fake. I was coming to realize he really did like everyone, think everything was great, and was happy to do whatever he could for you.

"Is Alice home yet?" I asked.

"She's taking a pre-party nap," he answered, looking out the window at Elliot.

"He's going to kill himself up there," I said.

"He loves to make her happy. He does all of her dirty work."

"Ouch!" I didn't think he was capable of cattiness.

"Sorry." He kept on dicing.

"Smells really good, Jay. What are you making?"

"Vegetarian paella. It's for tonight."

"It's good to be home again, where I can actually eat something at a party," I said. Our parents were vegetarians, and all three of us Harding girls were too, although Lacy considered bacon a vegetable.

I crawled onto my sister's bed and woke her up by putting little pieces of her hair in weird places until she smacked at herself.

"You're such a dick," she mumbled.

"You're drooling on your pillow. I'm trying to save it."

"What are you wearing tonight?" she asked.

"I don't know. What do you have for me?" I said, opening her closet doors.

"You'll stretch it out, fat ass," she said as I held a little black number up.

"Who's the dick now? I think I'll sit down a lot in this." I slipped the dress on and squatted down, sticking my rear out. I knew this was driving her crazy. My married butt was definitely larger than her newlywed butt.

I didn't feel like a party at all, but the candles were lit and the music was on. The ice was delivered, and the bar was stocked. The residents were gathered in the courtyard, and the slow chatter of celebration would rise as each new guest appeared. It was a gorgeous, clear evening. The lights were on in the cottage—the party pretty much took place at its front door. It would be very awkward if you lived there and didn't like to celebrate.

Everyone in the courtyard was wearing a hat. From the balcony, the scene was elegant yet comical. Well-dressed guests with colorful and, in some cases, sparkling heads.

Jason offered me up a party hat from a box they kept in the closet.

"Seriously?"

"She will freak if you don't wear one. It's a rule with her," Jason warned.

"You're lucky it's not October. She wouldn't let you have a drink unless you were done up. The same goes for the party hat on her birthday," Alice added.

I chose a handmade cardboard-and-newsprint tiara that had a tall crown and lots of silver glitter around the edges. It tied with a silver bow.

"That's my favorite. I made it," Alice said proudly.

"Very cool, dork," I said, putting it on.

Alice went to the refrigerator and grabbed two caramels. She handed me one. "You're going to need it," she said, then laughed.

"I can't! I am still drunk from today."

"Eat it," she ordered. "I never get to see you. You can sober up when you go home."

I did as I was told.

Jason was wearing a royal-blue fur lodge hat with horns coming out the sides.

"It's my standard," he said and smiled.

He looked like a cartoon Viking.

"Hilarious," I said. It was the perfect hat for him: fun, yet masculine.

Alice was wearing a traditional cone-shaped hat, but made of satin silver with large rhinestones around the base.

"Lee!" Sam Larkin, the older, more serious side of the Elliot-and-Sam couple, was the first to greet me at the stairs. He looked smaller than I remembered. He was still wearing an expensive suit, reminding me that it was a weekday. The fit was perfect on his almost frail frame, but the lapel and shoulders were slightly shiny from wear. His black leather cowboy hat was covered in studs. He had cool gray eyes. When you looked at him, something in you softened. He was a calming presence with a hint of a smile stuck on his face: a kindly observer of life. I guessed he was fiftyish.

"Elliot." He pointed at his hat. "Classic Castro. Just don't take me to the YMCA." He grinned.

My husband and I had a blast with Sam and Elliot at Alice and Jason's wedding (and the festivities leading up to the event). I was truly happy to see him again but was distracted by the shiny object to his left: Sophie Despre in a stunning red wrap dress, not a trace of underwear line or roll in her smooth, curvy lines. I sucked in my stomach and stood up a little taller. She was wearing a red-jeweled tiara. Alice called her "the Princess," which was fitting. I looked for damage from last night but didn't see any. Sam and I caught up on my kids and husband, and then I made my way over to Sophie, who was talking to Dr. Dan.

She was a mesmerizing, dark-haired beauty. Tall and curvy with big dark brown eyes, she was always made up with layers of lashes and perfectly applied black liner. Her lips were noticeably large, the kind you hated as a child and grew to love when you learned their power. She was in full control of them now, and they were painted as red as her dress. She could lose her Southern accent or lay it on good when she wanted to charm. Tonight it was on.

I had issues with women who didn't have women friends. Sophie was one of those. Women were only on the radar when they were useful. Alder was the perfect setting for her until Alice moved in. Now there were two princesses in the palace. She basically pretended Alice wasn't there, and in times of forced acknowledgment, tended to be snide and unwelcoming. If they were all getting together, she would invite Jason and not mention it to Alice, even if she'd seen her. And she had hit on him more than once since their wedding. I'd heard all the stories, so I was not a fan. I wondered if she knew I didn't like her, then decided she was too self-involved to care.

I'd beat her too, I said to myself and laughed in shame.

Sophie may not have been impressive to my sisters and me, but she was quite the businesswoman. She'd built a career for herself at one of San Francisco's once-booming investment banks. She was all over my husband at the wedding when she found out he was in finance, but I had stayed invisible to her. No need to network with the housewife.

She was one of those touchy people who feigned intimacy and touched my arm as she introduced me to Dr. Dan. She would have no problem holding my hand but would never know how many kids I had or what I did for a living.

Dan was the only Alder resident who hadn't made it to the wedding. I'd met him once in the courtyard briefly, but he was easy to forget. Tonight he was wearing a Giants baseball cap with a string of glittery thread wrapped around the base. He was wearing clogs.

He gave me a soft, wet handshake.

Dan's face was milky and clean with the exception of the mole on his cheek. His fine blond hair protruded from the sides of the hat. His thin lips were cherry red against his pale skin. The doctor's demeanor was benign, as if he didn't exist at all. He was average in height and thin but not skinny. He was wearing a short-sleeved, plaid, cotton shirt and bone-colored khakis.

Sophie was telling us a story about something funny that happened to her. Myles Alcazar made his way over to us.

"Wasted Wally is here," he said, not exactly whispering.

Myles was cute for a short guy. I was five foot nine and taller than him. He compensated by being incredibly buff. His dark hair and smooth Latin face were attractive, but I could see that something was amiss in his dark eyes. He was tightly dressed in a shiny black polo and matching flat-front slacks. I could smell hair product and cologne. His grooming was a contradiction to his merchant marine status.

Wally came in, and it was obvious he'd already had more than a couple of drinks. When Sam tried to introduce us, Wally made a joke about picking me up at the bar yesterday. He was a pocked-face big boy who hadn't figured out he'd left the frat house. It appeared he had not combed his hair since I saw him last.

I'd sat next to him and his wife, Diane, at the wedding. She was a kind woman who told stories that weren't true to help her cope with her miserable life. He spent most of his time at the bar instead of with her and their daughter. She spent her time imagining a different kind of life.

Wally liked to hump the leg of any woman who gave him a hello. He was Martha's nephew, so he was tolerated by the others, but barely. Jason was the only one who liked him. He worked closely with him at the bar and still liked him, so I figured there must be something more than what I saw. He was wearing a plastic beer hat, the kind you see on college kids and fat guys at football games. It had cups on the side and tubes going into his mouth so he didn't have to lift his hand to drink. His collar was crinkled, and his khakis had stains. The guy was a disaster.

"Shhh. Martha wants a dramatic entrance," declared Elliot. "A diva must have her day." He looked hot in a tight black T-shirt and black jeans. Perched on his head was an old-timey sailor hat that reminded me of Donald Duck.

When Martha finally emerged, it was in a gorgeous silk kimono, her red hair dyed with youthful brilliance and held up with lacquered chopsticks. Around her neck was a strand of jade beads weighted with an enormous centerpiece of carved jade. There was a burst of applause and shouts of "Happy birthday" as she made her appearance. Her flock surrounded her with compliments and hugs.

She was not wearing a hat.

Jason, who was acting as both bartender and DJ, raised the music a few decibels, and the party officially began.

Being the stranger in the crowd allowed me to sit back and observe the group. I watched Martha as she made her way around the party like a celebrity, gliding from guest to guest in her silky kimono. Her posture was that of a young woman with good manners. Everyone, including me, got the proper hello and was made to feel special in her presence.

"I needed a nap after our little party this afternoon," she told me.

"Yes, I'm feeling a bit hung-over," I told her. "Thank you for having me. It was a lovely afternoon."

"Let's do it again tomorrow." She winked and continued with her rounds.

Sophie heard us talking and came to me as soon as Martha was out of range.

"She dragged you into her lair today?" she asked, rolling her eyes.

I heard the words my sister often said to me when I did something that bothered her, like wearing a sparkly barrette in my hair, or wearing shoes she didn't like: "I will slap your face," she would say. It always made me laugh hard, but now, I really wanted to slap Sophie—with words, of course.

"The opposite is true, Sophie. She had to shove me out. Did she show you the poem Allen Ginsberg wrote to her?" I have no idea why I said this. It just came out—a complete lie.

She looked puzzled. I wasn't sure if it was because she knew Ginsberg was gay or because she didn't know who he was. I felt like such an ass. My sister would have come up with something so much better. I looked around for her and walked away, laughing to myself.

The men where sticking together. Myles, Sam, and Jason spent the evening chatting it up by the bar. Wally was there too, talking above the rest of them, laughing a little too hard. Dan sat at a table near them, but alone. I had the feeling that he was familiar with being invisible—maybe so familiar that he didn't even recognize it. *If he disappeared, would anyone notice?* It hurt my heart a little bit. I looked for sadness in his eyes but saw nothing. He noticed me watching him, and I moved on.

Sophie spent no time with Myles during the party except for a quick lean-in and a kiss while she graced the guys with her presence. It was as if nothing had happened the night before. I couldn't look at either one of them without thinking about what I had heard. For most of the party, she and Elliot walked arm in arm, making their way around the courtyard.

Several more neighbors and friends showed up. I thought it was odd that no one of Martha's age had been invited. Was she the last of the party girls in her generation? *Sad, that someone has to be left behind.*

A long table was covered in platters of beautifully displayed foods, some prepared by the Alder residents, some catered. There were dozens of flickering candles on every flat surface, including the bar. I looked up at the trees to see their tiny white lights intermingling with the stars displayed across the unusually clear night sky.

The caramel was kicking in, so my mind and body were incredibly tuned in to the magic of the surroundings. The rhythm of the music seeped into my being, and I was a part of it. I was aware of the calm of my breath. The sky was amazing, and I was aware of life's gift. This was what some people referred to as being present. It was not something I could do without help.

"Hey, stoner." Alice was by my side. She had caught me stargazing and was laughing.

I laughed too. "You can't imagine how good it feels to be outside," I said, trying not to think of the arctic weather I'd left my family behind in.

We watched as Sam took Martha by the hand and the two danced to an Ella Fitzgerald ballad. She was beaming from the attention and danced with graceful steps while Sam whispered something that made her laugh. A few people joined them. When the music stopped, Elliot brought out a gorgeous cake decorated with bright orange koi fish and black Asian lettering. We all sang "Happy Birthday" to Martha.

"It says, 'Our Queen,'" he said. "It's for you, not me," he added, and everyone laughed. It was an extravagant cake for a birthday party. But Elliot was an extravagant guy.

Most of the nonresident guests were leaving now. I saw Sophie whisper something into Elliot's ear. He, in turn, mentioned whatever it was to Sam, who shook his head disapprovingly. Elliot rolled his eyes and returned to Sophie's side with his answer.

Wherever Sophie went, Dan's eyes followed like a mother watching a toddler at a pool party.

"He loves her," Alice said. "What a fool."

I couldn't find it in me to feel sorry for him. She was obviously so far out of his league it was ridiculous. Clearly this was something he was unaware of. He didn't hold himself like a confident man, but he sure seemed to watch her like she was his.

Wally and Jason were talking at the bar, and I wandered back over to them in time to hear Wally vent.

"Look at her. It's not about her, so she is dying to get out of here," Wally said, watching Sophie with acidic eyes.

Wow, there was one man her charms didn't work on.

"Not a fan?" I asked.

"She's a venomous snake," he stated flatly.

I could imagine what their first meeting was like: Wally giving it his best shot and Sophie blowing him off with sharp insults. He had nothing to offer her. She probably didn't even bother saying hello to him on a regular basis.

Not long after, Martha began her good-nights. Kisses and hugs followed. Sophie tried to keep her from going, but she departed insistently, saying, "I can't keep up with you young people." I shook my head involuntarily as I watched.

"Let's go to the Jupe," Sophie announced before Martha's door closed.

Wally rolled his eyes and said, "See!"

"Come on. Sophie needs some outside attention," Myles said as we all headed down the alley to the Jupiter.

"You could have waited until she went to bed to bring it up. It is her goddamned birthday!" Sam said to Elliot under his breath as we walked to the corner.

"You got me in trouble, Sophie," Elliot said, apparently not taking Sam's scolding seriously.

I was so tired, but Alice convinced me to go for just a little while. We could hear the noise from the bar in the alley.

The Jupiter was full tonight. The crowd was made up of dot-com and college-aged kids.

"This place used to be dead until we moved into the neighborhood," Sophie told me. She walked in as if she owned the place and gave the bartender a kiss on the lips.

"Oh yeah, you made the bar successful, Sophie," Alice mumbled.

"Turn it up, baby," she ordered.

The handsome young man behind the bar obeyed her orders and poured her a glass of champagne. She took the bottle from his hand and left the glass.

I watched Wasted Wally living up to his nickname, slobbering all over some resistant girl. As he spoke to her, I could see her pulling back as if his breath was dragon fire.

Dan sat alone at the bar, watching Sophie have her fun. She was now hooting and dancing with Elliot on top of the bar. Young people shouted and clapped, and a drunken girl tried to climb up on the bar but stumbled down. None of it was for me.

I walked my weary body back to the apartment with Alice, Sam, and Jason. Sam turned some lights down, and Jason, Alice, and I went upstairs. My body sunk into the bed as I vowed to sleep until noon tomorrow. I just needed one good night of sleep...

CHAPTER 7

A NIGHTMARISH WAILING AWAKENED ME.

"Nooo! Nooo! Nooo!"

It took me a few moments to realize I wasn't dreaming. Once my eyes opened and I sat up in the darkness, it was obvious it was coming from the courtyard below.

The wailing continued as I stumbled out to the balcony. I knew that sound. I hated that sound. It could only come from death. It brought back my own sorrow in a rush, and I tried to push it down, but I felt sick.

Jason was soon next to me.

"Call 911! Call 911!"

The sound of Elliot's cries were horrific—the kind that only sudden loss could bring.

Sam ran by in his pajama bottoms.

"Nooo! No one is going to see her! No one! Do you hear me?" screamed Elliot.

"Let Dan in, Elliot. Let him take a look," Sam said.

"No! She wouldn't want him to. She's dead. Trust me," he sobbed.

No one forced the issue. Dan didn't seem eager to go in—just the opposite. He hung back as far as he could without leaving the scene, like that would make him disappear.

By this time, Jason and Alice had stumbled out to the door, and we all made our way downstairs.

"Someone killed her!" Elliot cried, continuing to block the door with his collapsed body.

My instincts were to leave the courtyard. The sorrow was too much for me. I knew that it wouldn't go away—you couldn't kill it; it was indestructible and had a very long life expectancy.

Everyone was in the courtyard now. The shocked silence suffocated the group. Elliot's crying had turned to moaning. The moments were painful as time slowed. The residents stood uncomfortably as the two men huddled at the door, Sam holding Elliot in his arms like he would an inconsolable child. Groans turned into shaking breaths, then slow sobs, then the moaning cry of pain again.

Jason suggested we give them some space, so we backed away to the tables. Myles had his arm around Sophie, who now cried quietly. Dr. Dan sat by himself at the same table, looking down at his fingers. I sat next to Jason and my stunned sister.

"It can't be true. She can't be gone," she whispered in the calmness of the aftershock.

"I'm going to wait in the alley for the police so they can get in," Jason said, heading out. I put my arms around my sister as she cried gently, like she didn't want anyone to hear her.

For some reason, I thought of this ongoing joke Alice and I had—a weird, sick joke. I would send her a photo of something really gross that I'd found online, like a guy with his guts hanging out at the scene of a car accident. I'd title the e-mail, "Max's First Day at School," or something sweet like that. She would wait a few weeks, then send me an even more violent photo with a subject like "The Perfect Sunset." I would open it unsuspectingly and find a photo of a decapitated woman. Finding humor in death and funerals was what we did to cope. So much easier than feeling the pain.

Jason led two uniformed officers into the courtyard, then two more paramedics. They all entered the apartment, and I held my breath, like she might still be alive. One of them came out and said, "Call the coroner," to a third cop, who had shown up last. The cop who had entered the house was visibly disturbed. A man in a sports coat and tie came shortly after that. He had a young but serious face. He went into the house with another plainclothes officer, a big-headed guy who looked like he was born to be a cop.

"I need a drink," I said to Jason. He brought me a bourbon and I drank it quickly.

Several members of a forensics team showed up with cases and equipment and white jumpsuits. The detective came out of the apartment and looked around. We were a sorry bunch. Half of us were in pajamas, myself included, and half were still dressed from the party. Sophie's heavy black mascara ran down her face. She looked like a vulnerable teenager in Myles's arms.

"I am going to need to talk to each of you," the detective said. "Has anyone left since the body was found?"

"No," Sam looked around and answered.

"Let's start with who found her. I am assuming it's you." The detective looked at Elliot, who was sitting on the ground against the wall of Martha's apartment.

"We had a party here tonight. It was Martha's birthday," explained Sam. "Martha Byrne, the deceased," he said to the fat-headed cop taking notes.

The detective looked again at Elliot, who spoke softly.

"We came home from the Jupiter. I was checking to see that the lanterns had all burned out. I noticed her door was open…" He broke off crying but mustered up. "She usually left it open a crack during the day but never at night. I pushed it open and called for her, thinking she was up, but the lights weren't on. So I flicked the light on, and there she was. Oh my God! Who would do this to her? Oh my God!" Elliot cried into his hands.

"Did you touch anything else?"

"No. Nothing." He was holding his face in his hands while he spoke, looking at the ground as if it would show him the answers. "I touched the light switch," he added.

"Someone must have come in while we were gone," Sam said.

I looked down the courtyard toward the old carved door. It was locked when we came back, and I saw Jason close it behind us. "The door was locked when we left," I said.

"And you are?" asked the detective.

"I'm Lee Harding. I am here from New Jersey, visiting my sister."

"Who is your sister?"

"Me," Alice said.

"How do you know the door was locked?" He was looking at my clothes, which were really my pajamas, a tank and a pair of black yoga pants. My long hair was tangled and loose around my shoulders. I was suddenly aware that I didn't have a bra on. I crossed my arms over my chest.

"Because I'm paranoid, so I watched, Mr....?"

"Healy. Detective Erik Healy."

"Mr. Healy, I'm nervous about safety when I'm in the city," I said. "When I grew up, this wasn't a great neighborhood. So I watched. I saw Sam shut the door when we left. I saw Jason unlock it when we came in tonight. He also closed it once we were inside."

Detective Healy was tall, but I would be taller in a pair of pumps. He didn't strike me as a man who would mind that, a woman being taller than him. He was fit but not thick-necked or busting-out-of-his-shirt fit. His sports coat hung nicely. I'd always preferred a man who understood that repetition was better than pounds at the gym, maybe because I grew up around the surfer body, which was lean and strong at the same time. I looked at his hands. They were large, and I felt a rush of blood at a very inappropriate time.

"It's true. I unlocked it when we came in from the Jupe," said Myles.

"Maybe someone climbed over the building and came down the trees?" suggested one of the cops.

"No way. There's barbed wire over the front of that building." Myles pointed toward the wall behind the cottage. "This place is a fortress. I've thought about it a million times."

I looked up and around at the square of walls that surrounded the courtyard. In order for someone to break in here, they would have to have serious motive, like a velvet pouch of diamonds, or Martha's painting. If that were the case, why wouldn't they just tie her up and leave her there? If a stranger committed the murder, there had to be a powerful motive to come into the intimate space and risk detection from the tenants.

"Why is that, Mr....?" asked Healy.

"Alcazar. Myles Alcazar. I'm a merchant marine. I'm gone a lot. I've thought about Sophie's safety here, and I've always been convinced this place is as good as it gets. Inside the door anyway."

"Are you saying one of us did this?" asked Elliot, looking up from his hands. "So Martha opened the door to someone she knew and..."

"Met a very violent death," finished the detective.

It was awkward while the residents looked around at each other with suspicion.

"Detective, is the painting over the fireplace still there? The nude?" I asked.

"Yes, it is. Why?"

"I was just thinking that if it were robbery, that painting would be gone. It's a Jean Claude Beaudin, and it's priceless. Unless it was just some junky..." I was thinking out loud. I didn't believe for a second that a drug addict scaled the walls of a warehouse, made it over the barbed wire, and scaled down to rob Martha for pocket change, killed her violently in the process, then left undetected.

"Anyone we should notify? Next of kin?" the detective asked. He'd listened to my comments but was not going to remark on them.

"We were her family," said Elliot. "Her husband died five years ago, and they had no children."

"There's Wally," Jason added.

"Who's Wally?"

"Wally McCourt. Her nephew," answered Elliot.

"Does he have a key?"

"Yes. He used to live here, in her apartment, before she and Harry moved down. Then he helped with the upstairs apartment renovations and lived in Alice and Jay's place," Sam said.

"She evicted him after Harry died. He never paid his rent," Elliot added bitterly.

"So they were estranged?"

"Not really. She felt sorry for him. He kept his job at the bar, and he moved in with his girlfriend, who's now his wife. Martha tolerates him. Tolerated him," Sam finished sadly, looking down at his bare feet.

Jason's face turned red with anger, but he didn't say a word. I thought about how hard this must be on him. He had known Martha for many years. She had been both mentor and mother to him, and he loved her dearly. He hadn't shed a single tear and was stoically caring for Alice as if she was the only one who'd lost something. Now his thoughts were on Wally—Wally the misfit, the man without a team, the man with a key to the courtyard, the man who was lucky to have Jason as a loyal friend.

"Can I get my girlfriend up to bed, Detective?" asked Myles. "She obviously didn't do it, and we are exhausted."

"Every one of you is a suspect, Mr. Alcazar. There are no obvious answers here."

"But we were at the bar and came back with Elliot. There are plenty of witnesses. I just want to get her to bed."

Sophie looked so vulnerable in his arms. The irony of fatherly protection was not lost. I imagined her on the bar, her dancing alibi. Myles was right; there'd been plenty of witnesses who would vouch for her.

"Honestly, Detective, we had a party here tonight. We were all drinking heavily. Can we do this in the morning?" Sam suggested.

An older man in a white coat came out of Martha's house. He motioned for the detective to come to him. They spoke softly. Then the older gentleman motioned inside the apartment, and two men carried Martha's covered body out on a stretcher. Everyone held their breath in silence for a moment, and then the quiet cries of reality became the background music of the courtyard.

"I'm going to be taking statements from each of you. I'll come back in the morning for additional information. After I talk to you, you can go back to your apartments. I'll have officers stationed at the door there and inside by the victim's door. No one leaves. Not for coffee, not for anything, do you understand? And no one is to enter the deceased's apartment."

We all nodded our heads like obedient school kids.

He started with Sophie and then Myles. Each of us was interviewed briefly: name, address, relationship to Martha, what we saw. Afterward, we were sent off to our apartments like zombies. I was so heavy with fatigue that my head and shoulders started to feel like lead bricks.

"Jackson, you've got the alley. Sanchez, come with me. We're gonna break the sad news to Mr. McCourt," I heard Detective Healy say as I practically crawled up the stairs to the apartment.

I sat on the unfolded bed. Alice climbed on next to me and lay down. Jason sat in the down-filled linen chair next to the couch, throwing a matching pillow onto the floor.

"There is no way Wally did this," Jason said.

"Why do you like that guy so much? He's such a d-bag," I said.

"He's not, Lee. He would do anything for his friends. He drinks too much, yeah, but he would go to bat for anyone he cares for. He was a disappointment to Martha, but he still would have done anything for her, and she knew it. He's honest, and he looks after that bar better than he does his own family. He loves the place."

"But it's not his," I said. "Maybe that's the problem."

"Well, it's going to come out anyway…" He hesitated. "She was selling the bar, Lee. But Wally had no idea. Elliot brought some investors in last week. I was told not to say a word, and I haven't until now. When it comes out, he is going to look even more guilty."

This explained Jason's earlier comment about Elliot doing Martha's dirty work.

"Word is out on the Jupiter, and it's making more money than it ever has," Jason said. "Wally runs it like the Irish pub of his ancestors, but the new crowd asks for cosmos and champagne, not Budweiser. Wally doesn't get that."

"I've never been so tired in my life," I whined. I didn't want to talk about murder anymore.

Jason stroked Alice's hair gently while she slept, then gave me a kiss on the cheek. "Good night, sleeping beauties," he whispered, then walked to his room, leaving Alice on the bed with me.

It seemed like only moments later when there was a knock on the door. I looked at the giant antique clock on the dining room wall and squinted until I could see the time. It was five a.m.

"Seriously? I just closed my eyes," I said, sleepwalking to the door.

"We need someone to let us into the bar," a uniformed officer said apologetically. "I understand Jason Martin has the keys."

I woke Jason up quietly so Alice could sleep.

I went with them down to the Jupiter. It was clear that I wasn't going to get back to sleep, and the curiosity of what they might find was hard to resist. Detective Healy and another cop were waiting at the door.

"We went to his house, but his wife said he never came home last night," said Detective Healy.

"Not unusual. He sleeps here a lot. He drinks too much. That doesn't make him a murderer," Jason said, switching the lights on and calling out for Wally.

"Wally. Dude, wake up," Jason said to the lump in the fetal position in the corner booth.

"That bitch," he mumbled.

"Dude. We have company."

"Hello, Mr. McCourt. I'm Detective Healy. We've been looking for you."

Wally sat up and scratched his dark mass of hair, which was flat on one side, curly on the other. He rubbed the crap from his eyes and said, "Wha'd I do?"

He smelled like a combination of the beer-soaked floor and sheets that hadn't been changed.

"First, why don't you tell us who you were talking about?"

"That bitch scratched me," he mumbled with a slur.

"Wally, dude. Martha's dead," Jason said.

Jason was looking at Wally's arms, which were marked with crescent-shaped punctures and scratches. Wally's acne-scarred face was blank. Like he woke up from a bad dream.

"What? What happened?" he said quietly.

"Where did you get those scratches, Mr. McCourt?" the detective asked.

"A girl. I don't know her. She was mean," he said, still confused.

I rolled my eyes at his stupidity.

"Wally, just ask for a lawyer. Don't say another word, okay?" I said.

"Thank you very much, Ms. Harding," sneered the detective.

Wally was taken away in a squad car for questioning. Poor Jason. I'd never seen him so upset. He was so faithful to his pathetic friend.

The sun was coming up as we were escorted back to Alder.

I went out on the balcony to see what was going on downstairs. About a dozen cops had assembled in the courtyard. They broke, and six came our way. I waited until they got to the top of the stairs and called Jason. They had search warrants for each apartment. They asked us to wait outside. Myles and Sophie came out to join us on the balcony.

"This is insane," said Myles.

Sophie was uncharacteristically quiet. I looked at her and saw a completely different woman than yesterday. Her hair was stringy and loose around her shoulders, her face makeup-free. She was still beautiful, almost more so without the mask of power.

I stood next to Alice, who was quiet.

I could see the others down below. Elliot looked like hell, but he was stronger than last night, standing on his own with his arms crossed, apart from Sam and Dan. Sam was reading his BlackBerry at one of the tables. Dan sat with a cup of coffee. He searched the balcony for a moment. Once he laid eyes on Sophie, he settled in with a periodical he'd brought outside.

The male cop, whom I recognized as Sanchez, came our way, accompanied by a female I hadn't seen before and Detective Healy, who was dressed causally after his all-nighter in a polo shirt and khakis. What a strange feeling it was to have someone go through my stuff. I hoped it was the woman who looked through my suitcase, which was open on the chair in the living room. I had underwear in there!

"Erik, what about this?" I heard Sanchez say.

Detective Healy joined the officer at the refrigerator.

"Oh shit!" I whispered to Jason. "The caramels!"

"So what? She has a prescription," he whispered back.

The detective said something, and the officer put the bags back in the refrigerator and closed the door.

They came out to the balcony.

"So I guess you don't think Wally did it either?" I asked the detective.

"Either?" he asked back.

"Well, my brother-in-law is pretty convinced that he isn't capable of murder."

"Everyone is capable of murder, Ms. Harding," he said stiffly.

"I don't know if I believe that," I said. "I don't think Gandhi was capable of murder. Or Martin Luther King." I saw the female officer's eyes roll. "Personally, I am not capable of murder." I felt like an idiot now but stuck with it, even if it was a lie. I would kill for one of my children. If someone hurt them, I would probably grow long claws and become a predator, seeking the perpetrator out and slashing them without hesitation. I was picturing my sleek, furry body walking through a dark neighborhood when I looked at the detective and saw him smiling a little. I felt stupid and hoped he wasn't some kind of mind-reading cop.

"Have you seen anything unusual going on around here since your arrival?" he asked me.

"No. Not really…"

"What do you mean by that?"

"Honestly, Detective, and I mean no offense to you, Jason, but this place is like a cult. The people here are very tight and more than a little dysfunctional. But from what I can tell, everyone adored Martha. She was the anchor for this little group," I said. "And she was a very lovely woman," I added.

"So you knew her?" he asked.

"Not really. I mean yes. I'd met her a few times, and well, I actually had a nice visit with her yesterday afternoon in her apartment. She invited me to come down. I brought a bottle of wine, and we shared it." A thought occurred to me. "She wasn't poisoned, was she?"

He laughed. "No."

"What did the two of you talk about? Did she seem nervous or upset about anything?"

I took a minute to think back, then said, "No. I admired the portrait in the living room. I guess you saw it. We talked about her years in Paris and how she got here. She told me about Harry, her husband. We talked about my kids, New York City—which she loved. Nothing else really. She invited me to come again today," I remembered sadly.

"Did she mention the Jupiter?"

"Not to me."

"What about you?" He looked to Jason.

"I think 'Happy birthday' was the only thing I've said to Martha in the past few days. I've been working a lot lately. I should have spent more time with her. I didn't get to tell her how much I care about her... how grateful I am."

This was the first time I'd seen Jason tear up. He took a deep breath to shake it off.

Alice sat quietly on a chaise. The detective looked to her.

"Do you think anyone in the complex would have motive for murder?"

"Not really. I did take her to an attorney's office a few weeks ago. She was rewriting her will," she told him.

"We're looking for a copy of that right now. Seems Wally would have been her only living relative. Are you aware of who would benefit from her death?"

"No. Sorry," Alice replied. "I just drove her there, and then we had lunch later, but I wasn't going to ask about her personal business."

"The bar was hers, and Wally could work there as long as it brought in what it cost to keep it. That was the deal. The real problem is that it was making a profit. Elliot had a client that was interested in buying. He owns several upscale bars in the city and wanted to add it to his group," Jason told him.

"How did you know about this?"

"Elliot brought him in on Wally's day off. I was asked not to say anything. He said he was acting on behalf of Martha. The deal was they were to keep me and Georges. Wally had to go though. I guessed he wasn't pretty enough for their image." He shook his head in disgust.

"What was Elliot's relationship to Martha?" he asked Jason.

"Gopher boy."

"You don't care for him?" asked the detective.

"He's out for himself. No crime in that. What bothers me about him is that he does a lot for Martha but always makes a fuss about it so everyone can see what a dedicated friend he is."

"And what was in it for him? Martha selling the bar?"

He shook his head and shrugged. "Something, I'm sure."

Again, I was surprised to hear Jason talk about Elliot in this way.

"You both have my number if you think of anything else."

"Can we leave the premises now?" I asked.

"Need to be somewhere?"

"Anywhere but here."

He smiled and gave us our freedom.

They went down the stairs with the other officers, who were done with their searches.

"We need groceries. And wine. And I need to get out of this murder hole," I told Jason and Alice. Then I went to the fridge for another caramel. It was too early for a drink. Between the sleep and the death, I wanted something to take the edge off. I am a monster without sleep, so it was just a matter of time before I became a super bitch.

"I'll go with you." Alice kissed her husband.

He softly brushed her hair from her eyes and said, "You okay? I'm going to Wally's to check on Diane."

My phone was vibrating. It was Jack. I had to tell him what had happened, but I didn't need another Lacy on my back. He was going to say he was coming out here, and I didn't want him to.

"Hi, hon," I answered.

"Hey, how was the party?"

I filled him in on the situation. He went back and forth with me, and I was a little snotty because of lack of sleep. I could feel the weed kicking in and wanted to hang up and enjoy it.

"I'm fine!" I told him. "I'll call you when I know more, okay?"

We headed out the door toward the upscale grocery store, which really cracked me up and made me sad at the same time. I never would have guessed it around here. My friends and I spent our youth at the grungy clubs that opened down here because the rents were so low. The drinks were cheap, and the bouncers didn't look at your ID too closely. But it was dangerous. My girlfriend stayed behind with a guy once, and the next day she got a call from the police. The guy had been arrested for robbing and beating a woman to death. He'd had my friend's name and number in his pocket. Now there was an organic market and stroller pushers everywhere.

"I ate another caramel," I confessed to Alice on the way down the street.

"Holy crap. I'd be freaking out right now."

Time passed, and I felt myself lifted from the tragedy of last night. I wandered around the store with an internal giggle. Happiness. I had left my phone in the apartment and felt completely unencumbered. I chitchatted with the produce guy about the piles of fresh artichokes and told him he hadn't really lived until he had a bowl of artichoke soup at Duarte's Tavern on the coast. I took my time admiring each pyramid of shiny red apples and heirloom tomatoes and walls of greens. There were bags of champagne grapes, which we didn't see on the East Coast. I loved the tiny little balls of sweetness and gazed at them for a long time, really seeing their beauty. I had missed them.

While I slowly cruised each aisle, not looking for anything in particular, I found a section of balsamic vinegars. An entire section! I held a bottle in my hands and read the label, thinking it must contain an extraordinary ingredient. I forgot why I was reading it but was engrossed by the logo, so I continued to hold it amazement. It cracked me up, and I started to laugh. A woman standing nearby looked me up and down. I was the crazy woman in her pajamas laughing at a bottle.

I got lost in the wine labels and don't know how long I was standing there before Alice found me. I had been thinking of Martha, then Paris, and the words she had said to me yesterday about how short life was, how I should live it fully. I wasn't sad, or thinking of her death but rather the life in front of me. Streaming ideas of optimism were flowing through my mind.

"Are you getting wine?" Alice asked, laughing.

"So glad you found me. I would have stood here all day." We laughed hard, so hard that Alice began to cry again. I hugged her there in the wine aisle, in my pajamas.

"Thirty dollars for a bottle of vinegar," I said, breaking up the hug. "People all over the world live on thirty dollars a month."

"I know. It's crazy. They probably sell a ton of it too," Alice replied.

I went through the checkout line and left the store with two bags of groceries. I had purchased the delicate grapes, along with many other items in the store I found to be "beautiful." I could no longer remember what I had come for.

Jason said he would meet us in front of the store. I sat on a low wall separating the store from the parking lot. The early afternoon sun warmed my shoulders, sinking into my winter-weary skin. I watched each person who walked out, inventing lives for them in my head. I didn't get to tune out—or in, for that matter—very often at home. The walls of responsibility fell down around me here, and even after the events of last night, I was free.

A young woman wrestled with three kids and an overstuffed shopping cart. They ran all over her while she tried to get them to stay in the car. She lost control of her cart in the meantime, and it went rolling off and banged into a car. I thought about the chaos that reigns when you have small kids. I knew how that woman was feeling. Each one of the kids was so little with their thick, pudgy legs and tiny voices that still said the funniest things. I remembered how my youngest couldn't pronounce his Rs. We used to ask him what a lion said, and he would roar, "Wwwwaaaaw," in a tiny, little voice, and I would kiss him and kiss him. She just looked at me and shook her head, unaware that she was in the glory days.

"I can barely remember my kids being that small," Alice said. "I wish I could tell her to slow down and cherish it, but it's so cliché."

My kids didn't need me so much anymore. They used to never shut up. Now they answered me with one word. "Fine." Everything was fine. School was fine. Soccer was fine. The dentist was fine. I wondered what they were doing right now.

A car pulled up, and the driver rolled down the window and said, "Jesus, you two look like shit."

It was Lacy. Jason had called her.

"Lacy the buzz killer," I mumbled. We got into the car and filled her in on Martha's death.

"Do you know what happened to her?" Lacy asked.

"No, only that she wasn't poisoned." I kind of laughed. "It must have been pretty brutal though because Elliot wouldn't let anyone see her. He was really protective of the body...like a faithful dog."

"Well, jeez. There's going to be DNA evidence. Nobody gets away with murder anymore, do they?" Lacy asked.

"They're looking for something. They searched everyone's apartments this morning," I said.

We pulled into the alley. There were only two cop cars now. I exhaled and prepared to go back in.

"They violated my suitcase," I added.

"You guys are staying with me," Lacy said. "There is no way you're going back there with a murderer living there."

"I'm not leaving my home, Lacy," Alice said.

"You are coming home with me." She was trying it with me. It wasn't hard to understand. If the tables were turned, and my kids were in this situation, I would have said the same thing. But we weren't her kids. She had never been able to stop parenting us. Sometimes I felt grateful, sometimes sorry for her, but most of the time, it was just super annoying.

"Don't get me wrong, I understand why you want me to go with you, but I am not leaving." This was said with a firm tone, so she would know not to push it.

Even if I could leave Alice, I preferred not to. There was a murderer in our midst, and I had a free pass to explore the situation. No, I was not leaving the compound.

This was not my first experience with a murder. One of our neighbors was killed a few years back, when we lived in Hoboken. In a way, the situation was similar. I knew it had to be someone on our street. I'd seen neighbor suspect neighbor before. That experience had almost landed me in the morgue. Lacy knew the story and was that much more nervous about it.

"Oh, so now you are a super sleuth? Do me a favor and don't get yourself killed."

This was how it was with us Harding sisters. Sometimes we didn't even need to talk to each other to know what the other was thinking.

"You hate that you can't make me leave." I laughed and hugged her.

When we entered the courtyard, I noticed that there was a cop stationed in front of Martha's door. Detective Healy was still interviewing residents. Another cop was outside the cottage. I guessed Dr. Dan was being interrogated. That should be a short interview. The guy didn't have much to say about anything. I realized that I didn't really like Dan. He wore clogs and he had no balls. Two strikes.

Sam came outside just as we were headed up the stairs.

"Oh hey, guys. Hi, Lacy."

"How is Elliot doing?" she asked.

"He'll be okay. He can't get the vision out of his mind."

"What happened?"

"He's not supposed to say. But it was horrible. Someone really had it out for her," he said.

"How could they?" Alice was crying again. "Who would want to hurt her?"

Sam just shook his head.

Alice made little sobbing noises as she made her way to the door. Sophie came out, and the two women had a short, awkward hug.

Just a few days ago we were so excited about spending time together. This was not the trip I had expected.

CHAPTER 8

ALICE WAS PUTTING HER LAUNDRY away, and I lay on her bed and kept her company. She was asking me about my boys, and I fell asleep mid-sentence. I woke up groggy and confused about where I was. The apartment was dark and quiet, and there was chatter outside. The residents of Alder were gathered at the table in the courtyard, drinking wine and talking about the events of last twenty-four hours. The wake-like tone ebbed from sadness to light laughter and back like a shallow wave.

"Hey, stoner," my sister yelled up at me. "Welcome back."

"It was a nice reality," I replied.

"Come down and join us," Sam demanded with great warmth.

My hair was flat on one side, and my mascara was smeared. I didn't really care. I went down the stairs in my sweats and joined them at a table.

A glass was placed in front of me, and Sam quickly filled it with red wine. I was feeling like an interloper, but no one seemed to mind my presence.

"I can't tell what time it is," I said groggily.

"It's five p.m., Dummy."

"Did they figure out who did it?" I asked.

Alice almost spit her wine out, and Sam laughed loudly, but the rest of them looked at me like I was an inappropriate stranger. I was suddenly aware of my morning breath. Wally came into the courtyard just in time to bail me out.

Even I could not believe he had the balls to use his key to come in.

"Are you fucking kidding me?" yelled Myles as he jumped up out of his chair.

Sam grabbed him, and Jason headed toward Wally.

"Dude, what are you doing here?" Jason asked.

"I have every right to be here! She was my aunt!" Wally cried. He looked defeated.

"You don't live here. Get out!" Myles yelled.

"Who are you, Myles? You're a tenant! And an evicted one at that!" Wally replied.

"What the fuck are you talking about?" yelled Myles. Sam was still holding him back.

"What, you don't know you were evicted? She wanted your wife-beating ass out of here! If there is one thing Martha was not going to have around, it was a wife beater."

Myles looked to Sophie.

"I was going to tell you," she said in a low, almost frightened voice.

He was silent. Everyone was silent.

"I don't know what you're talking about," Elliot said to Wally. "But I know one thing. You don't live here, and until someone tells us you own this fucking place, you need to hand over the key."

"I didn't kill Martha! I loved her. She was the only family I had left. I know you think she despised me. But she didn't. She was trying to teach me something. She loved me," he was sincerely crying. I felt really bad for him.

Jason held onto him and led him out the door to the alley. The cop in front of Martha's door stood deadpan. Jason came back a short time later and placed a key in the center of the table.

"Evicted?" Myles said to Sophie. "When were you going to tell me?" He glared.

She looked at Alice like she was Charles Manson himself and said, "This is your fault. Why couldn't you just mind your own business?"

"Really, Sophie? You let your boyfriend kick the shit out of you, and it's my fault? You should get beat up more quietly so I don't have to listen to it then."

The others sat in silence and curious shock.

"Yes, guys, the Princess gets her ass kicked regularly," Alice said. "I couldn't bear it and told Martha, hoping she could talk some sense into the girl about kicking his abusive ass out. She told me she would handle it."

Sophie's big brown eyes filled up with tears, and she grabbed Myles by the hand. "I thought I could change her mind," she cried. "I didn't tell you because I didn't think she'd really do it." Elliot was sitting next to her, and she leaned into his chest while she cried.

"She's really turning the shit on now," I whispered to Alice.

It was hard to feel sympathy for her. The lack of kindness made her an incomplete woman. If she had known how to care for others, how to be a friend, or how to give, she could rule the world. The missing ingredient would keep her always wondering what was wrong with others, and I imagined her raising little mean girls like herself.

I looked at Dan. His fists were clenched tight, and his face was bright red. I thought his head was going to blow up. He stood and shoved his chair back, then walked into the cottage, closing the door behind him. No one else noticed. All eyes were on Myles.

"It wasn't a problem until you moved in," Sophie turned back at Alice.

"Sophie, I am a woman—and a feminist, okay? Do you know what a feminist is? You're supposed to be this intelligent, high-powered businesswoman. Where I come from, women don't stay with men who beat them. And men don't hit women, Myles! What the fuck is wrong with you two?"

Myles got emotional. I couldn't believe my eyes. He started tearing and then sobbing. He fell onto Sophie's lap and cried into it. It was so pathetic. He was an abusive, pathetic shit.

I wanted to say, "Poor little woman-beating baby," but I didn't, since I was a guest.

"Poor little wife beater," my sister said. I loved her for saying what I couldn't.

Jason frowned at her. She ignored him and drank her wine.

"So when were you supposed to move out?" I asked.

"I don't see how that is any of your business," Sophie hissed.

It really wasn't. I had to agree. But I really wanted to know. Did she kill Martha because they'd been evicted? Maybe she thought no one knew about it and she could get rid of the problem. Does anyone love their apartment *that* much?

"It's a good question, Sophie. I'd like to hear the answer," Sam demanded.

"Look, I've been studying like crazy for my CFA. That has been my only goal. Once I passed that, I was going to deal."

"What happened with Martha?" Elliot asked.

I had assumed that Elliot and Sophie were close enough to share everything—not so in this case. If Elliot knew nothing about the eviction, how the hell did Wally find out? If Martha trusted Wally over Elliot, there was more to the relationship than there appeared.

"She called me down to her apartment about a month ago. I brought a pitcher of sangria and was ready for another boring tale of her adventures as a beat poet groupie. Instead, she sat me down and told me I needed to kick Myles out. She gave me a lecture about feminism and how I could do without him. And she wasn't asking. It was 'Get him out of my house, or you both have to leave. Do you understand?' I love living here! What would I do without you guys? I was going to tell Myles before he left at the end of the month. I just figured he would have one last month here. You're his family."

"So you chose the apartment over me? Is that what you are saying? After everything I've done for you, you goddamn cunt!" He was revving up to beating mode. Sophie was visibly scared.

I hated that word and was revving up to beating mode too.

"How long did you think I would put up with it, Myles? I'm not sixteen anymore. And I make as much money as you do now. I don't need this. Martha was right. What kind of woman puts up with it?" She was sobbing. For the first time, I actually felt sorry for her. He had taken her in and raised her, provided for her, and made her who she was. But he didn't own her soul as he had assumed.

"Stay with us tonight, Sophie. You're not going back up there with him," Elliot declared.

Myles rose. I thought he would kill Elliot right then and there. Instead, he walked up the stairs with his head hung low and went inside his apartment.

"Damn, there's a lot of shit going on in this place! I'm going out. You want to come?" I looked to Alice.

"Sure," she said. She looked at Jason, but he waved her on. I could tell he felt like he needed to take care of these people. I wasn't sure he was going to be able to.

"Mom and Dad knew how to raise girls," I said to Alice when we hit the alley. "Can you imagine anyone hitting one of us?"

We both laughed. Alice's ex-husband, Tom, had smacked her once when they were first married. She walked into her son's room, came out with a baseball bat, and struck him across the back while it was turned. It didn't happen again. I knew we were thinking of the same story.

We didn't talk about where we were going, instead we headed straight toward the water, away from the bridges and toward Mission Bay. We passed the new ballpark and the decrepit old buildings worth millions that sat on the new Riviera of San Francisco and pushed open the black, crusty door of the Mission Tavern. This was where all three of us Harding girls had had our eighteenth birthday parties (they had generously served minors in those days). It was where my girlfriends and I had played Otis Redding's "Sitting on the Dock of the Bay" so many times that the longshoremen who lined the bar asked the bartender to take the song out of the jukebox. He didn't, and we continued to sit on the weathered Adirondack chairs on the tiny balcony of the upstairs bar. Wrapped in blankets we brought with us, we studied the gray dark of hundreds of foggy nights, loving that song of our souls. Tonight would be no exception.

"Do you think if we call Lacy she would come?" I asked.

"No. She and Michael have theater tickets."

"Bummer," I replied. "Do you remember my twenty-first birthday party here? Chris Rollins showed up looking so good in that blazer and those jeans. Mmm. I loved that guy. I wore my purple angora sweater and felt so soft and girly. He treated me like his kitty cat that night." I said this while looking deep into the dense fog, so thick you couldn't see off the deck to the water below. There was a magical blind silence to the night.

"And you disappeared with him, and Lacy thought you might have drowned. I finally had to tell her you were just getting laid. Ha!" We both laughed.

"Sophie killed Martha so she wouldn't have to move out. I am sure of it," said Alice.

"That prissy little thing? Come on."

"You saw how she got with me tonight. Did you see the look in her eyes?"

It was true that she could be viper-like.

"I thought she was going to spit venom in your eye." I laughed.

"I wonder how she did it," Alice said slowly, to herself really.

"She was up on that bar, shaking her skinny ass all over the place. There was no opportunity."

"She had to pee that night. We walk home to use the bathroom. They're really dirty there. Maybe she snuck out the back and then came back in."

"Dr. Dan would have noticed. He never takes his eyes off of her."

"You figured that one out fast. I said that to Jason, and he said I was imagining things. He is such a guy—they notice nothing when it comes to love."

"That is truth, sister. That guy gives me the creeps. Do you think he would cover for her?" I asked.

"Maybe..." She was lost in thought, staring into the wet gray nothing. "He's a really nice guy, Lee."

"You sound like your husband."

"Seriously. No one in that freaking place, including Jason, has given my organization a donation. Even when we said 'no gifts' at the wedding and suggested they donate instead. Elliot and Sam bought us a gift anyway, and of course, it was a ridiculous antique clock from Elliot's store. And instead of a gift or donation, Myles and Sophie did nothing. Dan couldn't make the wedding but still donated a thousand dollars. I mean, he didn't have to do anything, did he?"

"That is generous. What did Martha do?"

"Martha gave us a free month's rent, and when we went on our honeymoon, she made sure he was compensated for the time off at the Jupiter. Bartenders don't get paid vacation time. It was incredibly generous. She told us she didn't want us to go to Guatemala worrying about how we would manage when we got back."

"Wow."

It took a lot to shut us up. That was what our mother always told us anyway. Martha's kindness, her life, and her death had finally left us without words. Alice shed a tear or two, and we headed home. The thick night fog blanketed our sorrow.

CHAPTER 9

I WAS FEELING GOOD. WHEN I looked in the mirror, I looked like my better self, the one who washed her hair and put on a little mascara. The puffiness of travel and sadness and exhaustion had departed, leaving me satisfied with my reflection. I put a little lipstick on after blowing my hair dry, which was loose around my shoulders, making me hot. I twisted it around to one side and was about to tie it up when there was a knock on the door.

"Good morning, Detective. Don't you guys call first, or were you trying to surprise us?" I was only half kidding.

He smiled and I smiled back, the two of us standing there, awkward—it was obvious our pheromones were compatible because every time I looked at him I got that feeling. My blood just flowed faster when he was in front of me. He was wearing a nicely fitted dress shirt and flat-front khakis with a navy sports coat. It might have been the first time he'd seen me wearing a bra, or that was what I was thinking as he stood looking back at me.

I was embarrassed and looked away, opening the door wider to invite him in.

"Good morning. Sorry. I should have called first." He smiled like he understood that I was playing with him a little.

"It's okay. I'm joking. How can I help you?"

"Actually, I'm looking for Alice."

"Oh. Okay. Let me get her." I wondered if he could hear the disappointment.

I went to my sister's bedroom and whispered that there was a hot detective in the living room. We walked back together.

"We're going to be releasing the body soon. We found a copy of Mrs. Byrne's will. She had very specific plans but asked that you execute them," he told Alice.

"What? Really? I would have thought it would be Wally and Diane, or Elliot...Okay. What do I need to do?"

"The autopsy will be finished by Monday. The body will be released sometime in the afternoon. Here's a copy of her request along with her attorney's information. She can help you with expenses from the estate. Here are the keys to Martha's apartment."

Alice took the paperwork and the keys and set about reading, tears filling her eyes.

"I'm going to need to ask you a few questions," the detective said. "Is this a good time?"

Alice chuckled a little. "Sure, have a seat. Sorry about the mess. As you know, my sister is in town. I was really looking forward to her visit." She wiped her eyes.

She hadn't bothered wearing makeup for days, giving it up to grief. Without it, you could see the slight imperfections in her face, a spot on the cheek from too much sun, some freckles, her tiny nose a little red from crying. Alice had my father's eyes, big and the color of the waters off Key West. Whether they were blue or green depended on the tide. Today they were verdant, muddled by sadness. She was wearing a pair of jeans and a white V-neck T-shirt and was barefoot. Her bobbed hair hung in points around her cheeks, and she tucked one side back behind her ear in habit.

I rushed to fold the bed, shoving blankets, sheets, and all into the cracks, and threw the cushions and pillows on top.

"Would you like some coffee, Detective?" I asked.

"Sure, if you have some made."

He sat down on the chair, my sister on the sofa. I gave him a cup of coffee and sat next to Alice.

"Do you mind if I'm here?" I asked.

"No, I'd prefer it." We locked eyes when he said it. "Actually, I have some questions for you too."

I didn't really hear a word he was saying. I was checking him out thoroughly. This was a boy who didn't skip a shave or a shower. Not for any reason. A real rules guy. He was a regular at the barber, with that clean-cut cop-guy thing going, but it wasn't cut too short, which kept him from looking military and softened his resolute face. His eyes reminded me of a cloudless, big-sky day. I wondered if it was death or fear or stress that made his hair turn gray around the edges of his temples, but it was creeping into the rest of his dark hair and adding to the attraction on my part. I wondered if he'd ever gone night swimming naked or fucked in a public place, and I found myself having to look away.

"I heard you found my stash." Alice smiled. She loved to flirt, and more than that, to make a guy like Erik Healy a little uncomfortable.

He took it well and with a slight smile said, "Yes, I heard about your sleep problems." He looked at me and added, "Do you have sleep problems too?"

"It runs in the family," I answered.

Alice laughed, and Erik and I smiled at each other for maybe a second too long.

"You told me to let you know if I'd heard anything around here. There was quite a scene last night. I think you should know about it," I said, changing the subject.

It was then that I noticed Elliot up in the tree again. He was struggling with the same lanterns I had seen him hanging for the party. His body language said everything about what had happened. What had been a joyous chore was now frustrating, and he looked angry. Alice and the detective turned to see what I was looking at. Just then, Elliot's foot slipped, and in his struggle to correct, he fell straight backward off the ladder. It would have been comical had there been a mattress down below, but we all knew there wasn't. He disappeared from view onto the brick patio below. We rushed outside and down the stairs. Before we reached bottom, I could see him lying on his back.

Erik ran to his side and checked his vitals. He was lying perfectly still, and I wondered if he was dead. Sam came running out, and the detective asked him to be careful not to move Elliot's head. Then he pulled his phone out and dialed.

Emergency services were called again to Twenty Alder Street. Sam was determined to stay calm. He took a deep breath and did as the detective asked, trying not to fuss. Instead, he took Elliot's hand and said gently, "I told you it could wait. I told you," as if it would somehow reverse the damage.

Again I felt the awkwardness of waiting in that courtyard. There was nothing I could do to help, and I hated just standing there. It would have been rude to head upstairs, but that was what I wanted to do.

Elliot was coming around by the time the ambulance arrived. They stabilized his head and neck and then loaded him into the waiting ambulance. Sam jumped in back and off they drove.

"This place is dangerous," I said to Alice.

"Not until you got here," she replied dryly.

Wally had heard the siren and walked over from the bar. He looked nervously at Erik Healy.

"What happened now?" he asked.

"Hi, Wally!" Alice grabbed him and gave him a huge hug. She filled him in on Elliot's fall. "I'm sorry about last night. I felt so bad for you." She was focused on him, standing very close as only a female friend could do. She still had her hands on his shoulders from the hug.

"They think I did it, you know," he told her like a boy who needs a mother, looking at the detective like he was a dreaded school bully.

"I heard. Don't worry. The truth will come out. I know you loved her, and she loved you too. She told me, you know," Alice said gently. "I'm sorry I didn't come after you last night," she said again. "After you dropped that bomb about the eviction, I couldn't move. I was so surprised! You wouldn't believe the drama that unfolded later." She took a breath and then added, "How are Diane and the baby?"

"She threw me out. She's 'sick of my shit.' Nothing like your wife kicking you in the balls when you're down."

"She does put up with a lot of shit, Wally." She said it so nicely that he didn't flinch. "Where did you get those scratches?" she asked him, taking his arm now and looking at it. I thought she was treating him like he was "special." He didn't seam to mind.

"I really don't know. I can't remember much from that night. I have visions of a tall blonde though," he answered her obediently.

"Well, DNA evidence is a good thing. She would have had your skin under her nails, right, Detective Healy?" Alice asked, still holding Wally's arm but turning to look at Erik for an answer.

"We're looking into that," he replied. He wasn't going to tell us one way or another if he still suspected Wally.

Monotone people really freaked me out. My family was passionate. We laughed hard, cried hard, and got excited about the little things. I wasn't sure what to do with people like Erik Healy.

"I need to talk to you about the funeral, Wally," Alice said, leading him toward the alley.

I turned to Detective Healy and filled him in on the events of last night while Alice and Wally walked to the alley. I whispered, not knowing if the two coconuts upstairs could hear us. I started the story with the night of the beaten Princess, peaked with Myles calling her the C-U-Next-Tuesday word, which I really didn't like to say, and ended the story with a brief description of the loud and disturbing sex we could hear them having this morning through the open windows.

"Think she did it?" I asked, knowing full well I wouldn't get a response.

"I've seen people kill for less," he answered.

"They would be losing a way of life, not just an apartment. You can't find a place this cool anywhere in San Francisco for the rent these people are paying." Jason had told me what they all paid. Martha kept things well below market rate.

Alice came back in, and we returned to our spots in her living room.

"Can I get you anything? Scotch? A caramel?" I asked Detective Healy.

He laughed a little, and it felt good, like I had broke him. He took a glass of water instead. I didn't eat a caramel in front of him. I wouldn't have put it past him to arrest me for it.

Alice talked about her days with Martha and tried to explain that Martha and Wally weren't so estranged. She didn't tell him about the deal with the bar. According to Alice, Martha must have felt really pushed into it by Elliot and really only wanted to see what they would offer.

"I've seen the will. She left the bar to him. Maybe he knew this and wanted her dead before she could sell it," he stated more than asked.

"If Wally killed her, you would know. From what I have seen of him, he's incredibly sloppy. There would be evidence galore. I'll bet some girl he grabbed at gave him those scratches," I said. "What kind of evidence do you have?" I asked with a slight smile, knowing he wasn't going to answer. He didn't.

"Well, can you at least tell us if you found what you were looking for when you searched our apartments?" Alice asked.

"Well, if I had, I wouldn't be sitting here now, would I? Not that I don't enjoy the company."

When he left, I felt ridiculously disappointed, like he forgot to kiss me.

"I'd tap that," Alice said when the door shut.

"What?" I asked her incredulously. "You can't tap someone. You have to have a penis to 'tap that.'" I laughed very hard, so hard that my eyes were tearing.

"Oh, I didn't know that's what that meant." She laughed too.

"Think he ever loses control? He's such a robot," I said, wiping my eyes so my mascara wouldn't smudge.

"I wouldn't mind finding out."

I knew she was full of shit. She was insane about Jason. I'd never seen her like that about anyone but him.

"Well, he would probably lose control if you tapped him," I said.

I didn't say it out loud, but I was thinking that I wouldn't mind finding out either. Something about the way he handled me. That perfect dash of authority...

Alice checked in with the hospital. Elliot was awake now but suffering from a concussion.

"It's twelve o'clock somewhere, sister. Let's get out of this death trap," she said after hanging up the phone.

We stopped at the Jupiter to fill Jason in on the events of the morning. He made us taste a new concoction, and neither of us complained. Then we headed to the new de Young Museum and hung out at the empty band shelter in the park across from it, reminiscing about childhood memories in one of our favorite spots. A violinist busked inside the shelter. We clapped loudly for him after each song and threw money into his open violin case. He thanked us modestly each time.

There were no leaves on the trees in the grid-like park that faced the shelter. Since I was a child, these trees had been pruned to have short, stubby branches. When they bloomed in the spring, they were little balls of green on a trunk.

"Why do they amputate them like that?" I asked.

"I don't know. Never really thought about it," Alice said.

"I've only seen it done here in San Francisco. I guess there isn't room for them to grow fully in the space," I mused. "They look like little angry fists."

Lacy finished with an obligation she'd had that morning and met us in the park for lunch. She pulled a full spread out of a soft cooler. There was homemade pesto, fresh sourdough, a wedge of Humboldt Fog cheese, and a bottle of wine. She was still taking care of us and so well. She forgot the wine opener and rolled her eyes when Alice pulled one from her purse.

"It figures," Lacy said.

"I can't believe you forgot to bring one, Mary Poppins," I teased. This was my nickname for her. She was always the prepared nanny.

We let Alice grieve but turned the tears to laughter each time with outrageous comments that would really freak out an eavesdropper. That was how we rolled, us Harding girls—red wine antiseptic and a Band-Aid of laughter. It had worked every time. I was missing my kids and husband but was also sad knowing this perfect state of comfort I had with my sisters was temporary. I couldn't have both lives at the same time, and it was keeping me from complete happiness.

"I'd like to beat the shit out of that Princess," Lacy declared.

"Myles has that covered, Lace, and it's not working. She still has a stick up her ass," Alice said.

"Maybe Dr. Dan can pull it out for her," I said. "He's so far up her ass already; it can't be hard to find."

"Have you seen the way she plays him?" Alice asked. "She does everything but stroke his balls. The poor guy! He thinks he's cheating on her every time he brings a whore home. That's my theory."

"I know you like that guy, Alice, but I can't forgive the clogs," I said.

"He does wear clogs. So wrong. It's a doctor thing though," Alice said.

"It's shameful, Dr. Shame Love," I said. "And honestly, the guy's a little creepy."

Alice called Sam's cell on the way home. Elliot would be spending the night in the hospital for observation and, aside from a slight concussion, would be fine. Sam was home when we arrived back at the compound.

"Come for dinner tonight," Alice told him. "You shouldn't be alone."

CHAPTER 10

THE EVENTS OF THE PAST few days gave the courtyard a drab tranquility. I sat on my sister's balcony in the thick mist of evening fog, swathed in what I now considered "my blanket" while sipping a glass of bourbon. The cottage lights were dim. A soft yellow glow came from Sam and Elliot's place. The police had picked through Martha's apartment like a collector at an estate sale, looking for any indication of that treasured piece of evidence. The yellow tape was gone, as well as the officer who had been posted outside the door. A stranger would believe things to be normal.

Sam came up the stairs with a bottle of wine in hand. I looked at the label and recognized the bottle as Stags' Leap. I wondered if he knew what he had brought us—it was one of my favorite cabernets from one of my favorite regions. He was wearing a pair of flip-flops, a wrinkled plaid shirt, and worn jeans that would probably fit my twelve-year-old son but hung loosely on his delicate frame. His shortly cropped silver hair was thin, and his face wore the events of the past few days.

"How's Elliot?" I asked from my chair.

"He's bitching about having to spend the night and already gave me a full list of exactly which clothes to bring him in the morning, so basically, he's back to normal. He can't remember a thing about yesterday though." He grinned, shaking his head. "He's very lucky."

"That's great news," I said. "I can't tell you how scary it was to see him go down like that. I'm amazed he's going to walk away without any real damage."

"Sorry about your so-called vacation." He laughed.

"Yeah, not what I expected. Can't say it's been dull though."

We went inside where Jason was cooking dinner and Alice was gathering silverware and plates. The apartment came with a very unique dining table. Martha had salvaged two old iron sewing machines and used them as bases. For the top, she'd found a massive slab of marble. It came from an old South of Market bakery that had shipped its business overseas. I could only imagine how they got it up the stairs. It looked amazing on the rustic wide-plank flooring with the open stainless steel shelving on the walls. She had created the perfect Parisian baker's kitchen right here in San Francisco.

"You could put anything on this table, and it would look good," I said.

"Martha loved it. And whether we liked it or not, we were going to use it. I don't even think it would fit out the door," Alice said. There was a chuckle, but it was weighed down by the grief that came when mentioning the dead woman.

"Who do you think killed Martha?" I asked Sam.

"I don't know, Lee. It's hard to imagine that it could be any of us. She was so loved—family, really." His eyes welled with tears and so did mine. "She had such an impact on the people around her because she taught us how to really live, you know? Really live. She was the most alive person I'd ever met. And so generous."

My sister and Jason were both nodding in agreement.

"The first time I met her was at MacArthur Park. She and Elliot developed a habit of drinking there after closing time at his shop. She was so immediately warm to me. And interested in my life, you know? You meet so many people that only want to hear the sound of their own voice. She was genuinely interested in people. A week later we received an incredibly generous donation from her."

"How lucky that I got to know her a little better before...ugh, I still can't believe it," I said.

"She's left a hole in the earth," he added.

"Wow. That's so lovely. I want to leave a hole in the earth when I go," I said.

It was quiet except for the clatter of glasses and plates as Alice set the table.

"Where are you from originally, Sam?" I asked, changing the subject. It was an attempt to keep everyone from crying again.

"Portland. My parents met here, but my father died before I was born. My mom moved back to Portland and married her high school sweetheart. I came back for college. I was at SF State when Harvey Milk was setting the Castro on fire with his big ideas for the gay community. It was his death that made me want to go to law school."

"Sam is the founding director of the Bay Area LGBT Union," Alice reminded me proudly.

The Bay Area Lesbian, Gay, Bisexual, and Transgender Union did great work in San Francisco. Sam's office was in the Castro District, which was the first and largest gay community in the country, and the heart of the city's gay activism and events. After district supervisor Harvey Milk and Mayor Moscone were shot and killed in 1978, the area was made nationally famous.

"Just because it's safe to be openly gay in San Francisco doesn't mean it isn't a hard life. The Castro was hit hard by HIV/AIDS in the eighties and nineties. Organizations like Sam's are instrumental in education and prevention. Many kids from all over the country flock to the city's streets to escape the persecution they suffer in small-town

America. Sam's organization provides the kind hand needed to help these kids up," Alice said.

"Wow. You must see it all." I felt like an underachiever.

"We do. We see a lot of kids whose parents kick them out because of their sexual orientation. The goal is to keep them off of the streets and away from drugs and prostitution."

"It's amazing to me that a parent would rather their child be straight than be on the streets. I mean, really? Do you love your kid at all?" I was thinking about my own boys. The conversation was making me want to call them to tell them I loved them no matter what.

"Many times it's a religious issue," Sam said. "Parents think the child will go to hell if they 'make the decision to be gay,' as if it's a lifestyle choice. So they exercise tough love."

"Is that in the Bible? Tough love? Poor God. They sure know how to make him look like an asshole," Alice said.

Unlike me, Alice had a loose belief in a higher power. Lacy was the only one who held on to religion after we lost our parents. I had always believed that she did this more for the formalities than out of true belief. Lacy lived a life of doing what you were supposed to: the church wedding, baptism, communion, and catechism. To me, they were rituals. I hated rituals. I was fortunate to marry a man who felt the same way. So our kids were without religion—although Jack Jr. told me recently that he wanted to be Jewish. I suspected that this was because a lot of his friends were getting bar mitzvahed. Sometimes I felt bad about not giving them any traditions, but I couldn't reconcile lying to them about my own beliefs: that we are on our own—that kindness and compassion were voluntary yet important to our human character for no other reason than self-respect.

"They believe they are doing the right thing for their kids," Sam said. "I know it can be hard to understand, but that's because we come from a different culture."

"Because life isn't hard enough for them at school, their parents have to reject them too. So sad," Alice said.

"Well, that's why we're here. We show them there's a better future, that it gets easier." Sam smiled. "Elliot does great work for us," he boasted. "He's been through some of the same experiences as a lot of these kids. His father tried to beat the gay out of him; his mother tried to pray it out. He ended up on the streets. He speaks to groups for me sometimes, letting kids know that it does get better. That's not all we do though. We fight discrimination, educate the public, and fundraise. Lacy's done work for us too."

"Wow. I feel like the loser sister here," I said, thinking again of how I needed to step up my life.

"I know how you feel, Lee," Jason said, laying a large platter of roasted winter vegetables on the table: carrots, brussels sprouts, squash, and onions—all browned to perfection and mixed with potatoes and rosemary sprigs. He grabbed a little ceramic pitcher from the counter and poured what looked like a balsamic reduction over the vegetables.

"You need to open a restaurant, Jason," I said, my mouth watering.

He added a platter of sliced cheeses and a basket of sourdough bread to the table and smiled shyly.

"What do you do?" Sam asked me.

I was trying to think of something to say, but Alice answered for me.

"She's raising the future of our country while managing the household. It's a big job." She was always on my side. "Lee has a degree in economics. She graduated at the top of her class. She's almost done with the kids. Grad school next, right, Lee?"

"I'm not living to my full potential yet." Oprah had taught me that...and Alice. "I don't really know what I'm supposed to do when I grow up," I said. "My kids come first right now, but it's almost my time. I think I want to go to Columbia and study global affairs." It was the first time I'd felt good about saying this out loud.

"She's going to be the next Jeffrey Sachs," Alice said.

If ever there was a man Alice would leave Jason for, it was Jeffrey Sachs. Everyone who knew her knew she had a huge crush on him. We saw the celebrity economist speak at Columbia once when Alice was visiting. She cornered him after the lecture and asked him question after question, flipping her hair and smiling like he was a rock star. The guy was tiny and had the slicked hair and glasses of a class-one nerd, but women lined up behind her.

"Why, so you can stalk me too?" I asked, sharing the story of Alice at Columbia.

Jason laughed the hardest, knowing well about her obsession.

"I didn't know economists had groupies," Sam said, laughing.

Jason filled us in on the happenings at the Jupiter. Finally, he looked at Alice, prompting her.

"We need to talk about Martha's funeral arrangements. She left instructions for me to make them." She was obviously uncomfortable.

"That's fine, Alice. I'm well aware that Martha adored you. Do you think she would let just anyone move in here with Jason?"

Sam was consistent in his politeness—like a good English gentleman.

"Do you think Elliot will feel the same way? I know how close they were. I was very surprised and, honestly, a little pissed that she put me in this situation."

"She trusted you to do as she asked. Now what did she ask?" The lawyer in him got down to business.

"She wants her wake to be in the bar. We are to cremate her, then put her ashes in the dragon jar. Do you know what she means?"

He smiled. "I know the jar. It's the first thing she ever bought from Elliot. It will make him very happy. Jeez though, it doesn't have a lid."

"Well, there's more...the jar is to sit on top of the bar, and there is to be a party. I have a list of guests to invite and very specific instructions on how things are to be decorated. She also wrote her obituary for the *Chronicle.*"

"She was such a control freak." Sam laughed.

"She wants us to take her out to the Golden Gate. She left a contact for the Marina Yacht Club. A gentleman friend of hers will bring us. The coroner is releasing Martha's body tomorrow. We'll get her back from the funeral home on Wednesday," Alice said. She rolled her eyes toward the shared wall. "Can you let the Princess and the Beater know about the arrangements? I can't bear to look at either one of them right now."

"Sure," Sam said. "And don't worry about Elliot. He's a bit unraveled. I'm sure he'll be relieved that he doesn't have to deal with all of this. Plus, I'm going to be making him take it easy for a while."

While Alice and Jason prepped dessert, Sam and I settled into the sofa. He was kind and comfortable. We both had our shoes off, and I pulled my legs up onto the couch, facing him Indian style.

"It's hard to believe that a loony got in here, and I don't want to believe that there is one sleeping amongst us," I told him.

"None of it makes any sense to me. I wish I had answers." I watched him think about all that had happened. "I'm gonna miss that woman," he said. If he was lying about his feelings, he should have gone into theater. I was completely convinced.

After dessert, Sam gave us all hugs and returned to his empty apartment. My sister and I had one last drink while we curled up on the sofa. Jason kissed us good-night and headed to the bedroom. We talked about the next few days.

"I still can't believe she's gone," Alice said. "It just keeps coming at me like a wave."

"It's weird, but I feel like she somehow knew her time was at an end. She actually said to me, 'I was born yesterday and will be dead tomorrow,' or something like that. I can't stop thinking about it," I said.

"Gives me the chills." She shivered quickly, like a wind blew in.

"The fact that there is a murderer walking around gives me the chills," I reminded her.

Extra care was taken to bolt the doors and check the window locks that night. I went to bed wishing I were in the back of the house, like Alice and Jason. I fell asleep watching the shadows of the old trees outside the large front window in the living room.

CHAPTER 11

MISTY TEARS OF FOG WEIGHED heavy on the trees in the courtyard, dripping sorrow onto Sam and Elliot as they shuffled in from the hospital, Sam holding Elliot's bag, the latter moving slowly as if it hurt less. With the exception of a flushing toilet and some dish clatter, we hadn't heard a peep from the next-door neighbors since the Myles blowup and the obnoxiously loud makeup sex we were treated to later that morning.

The gloom of the dark air reminded me that the weather wasn't always great here. A cold wind was coming off the bay, and even though the temperature was in the fifties, the dampness caused a deep chill that made it hard to warm up.

Alice had the week off work, and Lacy came over with bagels. We sat in our pajamas and drank coffee in the living room. Alice and I had both had a caramel before Lacy's arrival, but it hadn't kicked in yet. Several minutes later, Alice said a coworker ran "buckshot" over her instead of "roughshod." Her battle with clichés was a joy, and I laughed very hard. Curled up in the chair in slumber-party mode, I could not have been more comfortable.

"Stoners," Lacy said when the laughter went on too long. "I don't understand why you want to make yourselves stupid on purpose."

"It's better than Xanax, Lace," I said. "At least it's not concocted in some lab, with side effects that include high blood pressure, brain tumors, and anal leakage."

Alice gave me a dirty look. I knew Lacy had taken antidepressants for a while, but I wasn't supposed to know. I couldn't figure out why it was such a big secret. All three of us had issues from the death of our parents, but to me, Lacy had it the worst. She'd lost so much of her childhood to becoming family leader, a burden on any oldest child, but in our case it was literal. I could see no shame in needing a little help to ease the pain once in a while. But Lacy was in the camp that said that marijuana was a drug, not an herb with medicinal effects or a recreational buzz, but a drug. Her camp also believed that if a doctor gave it to you, it was safer.

"It's nice to check out, Lacy. It's like therapy. You know that moment when you sit on the beach and watch the sunrise, and you think that life couldn't be more beautiful? Well, you kind of get stuck like that for a few hours. Want one?" Alice asked from the refrigerator.

"Maybe when we go camping," she said. We had planned a trip to the redwood forest before I had even arrived. "If I get paranoid, it will be your problem."

Alice and I looked at each other in happy disbelief. I was expecting her to tell me that we should learn how to have that feeling unaided, but I guessed she didn't want me to bring up the Xanax again.

We kept the conversation light that morning, but every so often it would turn back to Martha and there would be sadness. I made a "No Death" rule for the day, but it lasted about ten minutes. I didn't enforce it because Alice needed to talk it out.

Just before lunch, she said, "Come down to Martha's apartment with me. I need to get the jar, so they don't give her back to me in a cardboard box."

"There's no way I am going in there," I said.

"Please! I can't go alone."

"Make Jason do it," I suggested.

"I'll go," announced Lacy, taking control as usual. "Come on."

Once Lacy decided to go, I somehow felt safer and agreed to join them.

Alice grabbed the key Detective Healy had left her. She gave me some flip-flops, and we headed downstairs, both still in our pajamas. When she unlocked the door, she held it open and Lacy entered first. Alice turned on the lights, and I came in last, leaving the door purposely ajar so we could run if we needed to.

"I feel very weird about this," I said.

Lacy walked bravely down the hallway, turning lights on as she went.

"What a cool place," she said. "Vintage intellectual."

I followed her because I hadn't seen the bedrooms when last here and because I was super nosey.

"Whoa! Time warp," Lacy said when she saw the bathroom.

There was a small white wrought iron stool tucked into a white laminate-topped vanity. The sink, bathtub, and toilet were pink. Martha's cosmetics were laid out on the dressing table. I could imagine her putting on her makeup, not knowing it would be the last time.

"Weird," Alice said over my shoulder as we crowded in the doorway, peering in as if entering the space would be a violation of Martha's privacy somehow.

We followed Lacy to the larger bedroom.

"Her bed's made. She hadn't even made it to bed yet," I said. "Whoever killed her didn't wait long after we left for the Jupiter."

The wall parallel to the bed had navy wallpaper with delicately drawn camellia-shaped flowers, while the bedspread had the reverse pattern. There wasn't a wrinkle on the bed, and the pillows were tucked into the bedspread and folded over so as not to expose their intimate linens. My mother made her bed the same way. The rest of the room was painted the same dark navy color, even the trim and closet doors. A large white shag carpet covered the wood floor. I knew her side of the bed by the pile of books neatly stacked on the nightstand. Above the bed was a painting of a young man in a rowboat, reaching up to the low moon, obviously inspired by the Italo Calvino fable.

The second bedroom was used as an office. There were dozens of drawings, poems, and memorabilia nicely framed in black on beige linen walls. I noticed an article titled "The Beat Muse," yellowed from decades behind the glass. Next to it was a photo of Martha posing confidently in front of the City Lights bookstore. She was wearing a sleeveless mini sheath with horizontal stripes and Roman sandals that laced up to the knee. Her hair was straight and long, and she had bangs. She was thin to the point of lanky.

"Great dress," Lacy chimed.

"What a life. Mine is so dull in comparison," I said.

"I'd rather be boring than dead," Lacy reminded me.

"Live big, die big," I said. But as soon as the words hit my lips, I knew that I didn't mean them.

Eventually, I wandered back to the living room and faced Martha's portrait. I couldn't move—it wasn't just the buzz; the painting was really something. Alice soon joined me.

"She loved talking about Paris, and I loved listening," Alice said. "This painting says everything about who she was. What a cool woman. Everyone in town knew her. Her greatest secret was that she loved Perry's on Union Street more than her own bar. I went there with her once. She said, 'Want to go have a drink? Not a cocktail, no mixologists, a drink, at a bar, with bartenders.' When we walked in, the bartender asked where she'd been, like she was the mayor. Then he said something to the waitress, and Perry Butler himself came out and gave her a big hug, seated us, and bought us champagne. I asked, 'How often do you come here?' and she said, 'I haven't been here in at least a week.'"

Lacy came in from the hall and looked at the portrait. "Perky," she declared.

Alice and I started laughing, and then it was on; there was no stopping the wheezy tears that poured from our eyes. It was the kind of laugh that came from release. We'd learned to do this instead of cry.

"What's so funny, ladies?" It was Erik Healy, leaning casually against the bookshelf in the foyer and possessing a large grin. He was wearing a navy sports coat and a white oxford with jeans. His eyes were bluer than I remembered, and I thought he got more attractive every time I saw him.

His serious nature felt authoritative though, and it made me feel like a slacker. Alice started laughing again when she saw him, and that made it worse, and I ended up holding back laughter too. I felt like a child.

"Hi, I'm Lacy, Alice and Lee's sister. And you are?"

"Detective Erik Healy," he said, reaching his hand out to shake hers.

"Nice to meet you, Erik. We came down to get the jar for Martha's ashes. She requested a specific one."

"I see," he said.

Alice and I were so red-eyed. The tears were streaming down our faces from the laughter. We stood there in our pajamas—at least I had a bra on this time. The officer we referred to as Fat Head was standing next to him with the same condescending look I'd seen since he'd arrived here the night of Martha's death.

Please don't laugh, I thought to Alice. I knew she was looking at me. I refused to look back.

"Having some sleep problems, ladies?" the detective said with a smile.

"The last couple of days have been hard on them," Lacy the Protector stepped in. She would always make excuses for us, even when she disliked the behavior.

"Did you find the jar?" he asked.

"We hadn't really looked for it yet." I started to giggle, and so did Alice, who saw the jar on the corner table and grabbed it.

"Here it is," she said, spitting a little as she tried not to laugh and then managed to say, "It has no lid."

"Are you back to look for more evidence, Detective? We thought with the tape gone it was okay to enter," injected Lacy.

"We have an appointment with two of the residents. I heard noise in here, so I thought I would see what it was about. Anything I should know about since I saw you last?" He was looking at me.

"It's been pretty quiet around here," I told him.

"Okay, ladies, carry on." He smiled and left the apartment.

We stood there looking at each other for a moment in silence. I was starting to recover enough to talk anyway.

"You called him Erik!" I barely got it out. Alice and I rolled into laughter.

"It has no lid?" I asked when I could breathe again.

"Get dressed, stoners. We're going to lunch," Lacy commanded.

There was still silence upstairs, and the cottage lights were out, so I figured the detective was at Elliot and Sam's. After showering and dressing, we made our way down to the courtyard. Since I was the guest, my sisters deferred to me, so we were about to head to the Mission for a burrito. When Alice pushed the door to the alley open, we saw Myles standing there with Dan in a headlock. Dan was still wearing his scrubs—and clogs—and there was a bag of garbage lying on the ground.

"What the hell are you guys doing?" Alice yelled. "Let go of him now!"

Myles's cheek was already starting to swell.

"He fucking attacked me!" yelled Myles, not letting go.

"Let go now!" Alice commanded.

Dan was pathetically struggling to be released, swinging wildly. Lacy grabbed Myles, and Alice grabbed Dan, and they pulled them apart.

"I was emptying the garbage, and this crazy fuck just walked up and cold cocked me!" Myles was clueless as to why Dan would do such a thing. He was so self-absorbed that he was oblivious to how the angry doctor felt about his girlfriend.

"You hit her! You fucking hit her, you bastard!" yelled Dan, now in tears and shaking violently. "I will kill you!" He went at Myles again, but Alice and I both held him back.

"Dan, get inside right now. Go. Go!" Alice pushed him into the door and closed it. "You're so clueless, Myles. If you had your eyes on anything but your mirror, you would know that he is madly in love with her. When you're gone for months at time, who do you think she leans on?" Alice asked him without waiting for an answer. "And don't go upstairs and beat her for it. She uses him up. She doesn't give a shit about his feelings either."

He was rubbing his cheek like it smarted.

"And you might want to behave. There are two cops inside," she warned him.

We walked down to the Jupiter. Jason was working, and Alice filled him in on our morning.

"I'm having a drink," Lacy declared.

This made me laugh. It had to be her first ever before sunset, unless you counted a piña colada on a cruise once. She ordered a gin and tonic and drank it down fast.

"Shit, Lacy! Drinking problem?" I teased.

We walked by the office at the *Chronicle* to drop off the obituary and then caught a cab to the Mission.

The next day, the *San Francisco Chronicle* published the obituary Martha had written for herself.

Martha Swanson Byrne, loving wife of the late Harold Thomas Byrne, died February 22nd, 2008. She was the granddaughter of the late Tilton Swanson, silk manufacturing magnet from Paterson, NJ. She was educated at the Sorbonne in France.

Mrs. Byrne had a successful career as an abstract artist in the '50s and '60s. In her favorite review, a critic called her work "writhing with seduction." She was the muse of artist Jean Claude Beaudin and the inspiration behind the great poems of Johnson Wiley.

She did not wish to share her age, but wanted it to be known that she didn't waste a single day of her life.

She leaves behind a nephew, Wally McCourt, his wife, Diane McCourt, and their daughter, Tabitha, as well as members of her adopted family on Alder Street, her home since 1967.

A gathering will take place at the Jupiter bar on the corner of Alder and Brennan on Thursday at 7:00 p.m. Guests are asked to refrain from wearing black and should remember that it's a celebration, not an excuse to be boorish. Party hats are required.

CHAPTER 12

ON THE DAY OF THE wake we picked up the dragon jar with Martha's ashes. The funeral home was kind enough to create a Styrofoam plug to keep her remains from falling out. The walk back brought us through some of my least favorite streets. The wide avenues with numbers for names were lined with halfway houses and residential hotels for the city's drug-addicted and chronic homeless. A long line of men waited for salvation—or breakfast maybe—outside the YMCA.

Alice and I both feared dropping the honored contents, so Jason was in charge of carrying Martha back to the Jupiter. Wally cleared the liquor off one of the higher shelves, and there sat Martha, perched on her ledge in Asian attire once again.

"She needs a party hat," I said, but then remembered that she didn't wear one at her birthday either. "Or chopsticks maybe."

"Little Ms. Royalty better not dance on my bar tonight," Wally mumbled to Jason as he strung lights.

"She'll turn Martha's funeral into an event about herself for sure," Alice said.

We were decorating the bar with strands of little twinkle lights. For a woman who loved color, she had a very strict plan for a thousand white lights to be strung close to the ceiling. We spent the day tacking them up. One hundred colorful paper lanterns from Chinatown were found in Martha's storage closet and hung up as she had directed. Elliot was helping us as best he could from the ground—no one would let him up on the ladder.

"If this is how she wanted the bar to look, why didn't she just say so before she died?" I asked.

"Not sure this was Harry's vision of the bar, but I like it," Wally said.

"Is Diane going to be here tonight, Wally?" Sam asked.

"Yeah, she should be here," he replied. "She kicked me out, you know?"

"Sorry to hear that," he answered.

Who could blame her? That's what I was really thinking. Wally had been cleared of all charges relating to Martha's death. A witness came forward to say he saw Wally get the scratches from a girl he'd grabbed. His bad behavior had taken place during the time of death. That was the final straw for Diane, who didn't find her husband's groping alibi a relief.

I wondered what his mother did to him to make him such a perma-child and thought that being a male and an only child could sometimes generate overindulgence on the part of a parent. Most women I knew weren't interested in mothering their husbands. I felt grateful for my own spouse, who was playing single dad beautifully at the moment.

"One thing I've learned from all of this is that I need to get it to-gether. If I died tomorrow, what would my obituary say?" Wally said.

"Mine would say, 'We all end up dead, and so did she,'" I said.

"Jeez, Lee!" Alice shook her head.

"It's true. I'm not going to make up some flowery crap about life. We all end up dead. It's the one thing that we know about our lives— the ending to the story."

"Who knew you where so morose?" Elliot said. "I really do need to step it up though. 'Supplied antiques to San Francisco's nouveau riche' isn't going to cut it."

"Oh, come on, Elliot! How about, 'Helped hundreds of gay youth learn that there is hope and love in their future'?" Sam said.

Elliot was visibly touched and sent a loving smile down the bar where Sam was working.

"Life partner of a true hero," Elliot added sweetly.

"Enough. I'm going to vomit," Alice said, speaking my thoughts, as usual.

At seven o'clock sharp, while most people were still rushing to get ready for the event, a gentleman with a gray suit and black fedora entered the bar. The fedora had a purple feather protruding from the band, the older man's way of honoring Martha's request. His nose told me that he once did some boxing, and his large hands confirmed the story. He sat at the bar and ordered a gimlet, placing a twenty down in front of him.

"It's on Martha tonight," Jason said, pushing the money toward the old man.

He smiled and held his glass up. "Thanks, Marti."

He had a spirit of devilishness, like he'd grabbed a few rear ends in his lifetime—the type of man who used the words "dame" and "broad." I was sitting a few seats down and leaned over to say hello.

"Well hello, pretty lady," he replied.

I did feel great in my sister's crème V-neck T-shirt dress. It was silk crepe and would have taken itself far too seriously had it not ended abruptly above the knee. I scooted down a seat to be next to him.

"Lee Harding," I reached my hand out for a shake, but he kissed it instead.

"Francis Rogers. It's a pleasure."

"How did you know Martha?" I asked.

"Oh, we went way back. I met her at City Lights in '57. It was the same year *On the Road* was published."

"Wow! You remember the year?" I could barely remember the years my kids were born.

"You don't forget the important stuff. I was nuts about her. She had just moved from New York, chasing after that loser wannabe poet, Wiley. He was too smooth for his own good and couldn't appreciate a woman like Martha Swanson for long. He let her down hard, and I picked up the pieces. 'Course, once she fell for Harry, it was all over."

"How did she and Harry meet?" I asked.

"Well, that's a story," he said, shaking his head a little as if he still couldn't fathom it. "Martha had a friend, Jane, who lived in the same building. They lived on the fourth floor of this shabby little box on Green Street. Marti wanted it to look like she had no money. See, she was slumming there, but it was real obvious she was a classy gal. When the poet left her, Jane felt real bad and invited Martha to pal around with her and her husband. Jane was a nice gal. Her husband was a welder down at the docks. He thought of himself as somewhat of a poet too, but hell, we all did back then. His name was Harry Byrne. Anyways, Jane thought we'd be perfect together. Marti and I started seeing each other—I was mad about her—but she was just going through the motions with me. I figured she was still hung up on the phony poet. We did a lot of things together— she was always a real nice gal, and gorgeous. Even if I didn't stand a chance, she looked good by my side, right? We all went down to Mexico for a month that winter. One afternoon, Jane was taking a rest; she had a headache or something. Marti and Harry decided to go off to some beach that the bartender had told us about, but you had to hike to get there. I had a bum knee and decided to stay behind. They were gone a long time...too long. After that, it was obvious there was something going on. They were taking off to spend time together every chance they got."

He shrugged his shoulders. "These things happen. What can you do?" he said, letting me know that he wasn't making any judgment calls. "Jane finally called them on it when we got back to California. She stood up to Harry like a tiger. 'It's me or her. Choose now,' she said. He stuck with her for a while, trying to do the right thing. Marti went back east for a couple of months. When she came back, they still couldn't keep away from each other. Jane left Harry and moved back to her mother's house up north. She was pregnant at the time—that's what I heard anyway."

"Wow," I said. "No wonder she didn't want to talk about it when I asked."

I wondered where Jane was now. If that wasn't grounds for murder…

Erik Healy walked into the bar, and I felt like the evening just got a little better.

"Fancy meeting you here, Detective."

"Erik," he replied.

"Are you off duty?" I asked.

"An officer always makes an appearance at funerals. Since there isn't going to be one, I figured this would be the place to pay my respects." He was not wearing a hat but was all silvery and Wedgewood blue with his hair and eyes and tie.

"Where is your party hat?"

"I'm all out. I like yours though."

"You do? You do like my party hat?" I laughed.

He gave me a blank look as if he was trying to figure out if I was out of my mind or not.

"It's a line from a children's book, *Go, Dog. Go!*" I said. "Sorry. I've read it so many times I expect everyone to know it."

"Do you have kids?"

"Yes, two lovely, crazy, smelly boys. Twelve and fourteen."

"Wow. You don't look old enough to have teenagers."

"Thanks. I was fifteen when I had my first," I joked.

"That explains it."

"Explains what?"

"You're reliving your childhood." He smiled sarcastically.

"Oh, you mean the pot thing?"

He raised his eyebrows.

"Have you ever been to a rock concert? A really crazy hardcore concert where people are drinking up a storm?" I asked.

"Yes."

"Well, then you've seen what happens when people drink too much—fighting, puking, driving out of the parking lot when they shouldn't even be in a car. And you're a cop. How many times have you arrested people for being idiots or hurting others when they are drunk? Is that any better?"

"Too many to count," he said. "Look, I know where you are going with this. It's true that I don't think I have ever seen potheads fight. They are a lot more manageable in large groups than drinkers. But it's still an illegal substance. That's the bottom line."

"I hate that argument. Plus, it isn't exactly true here, is it?"

"Apparently it's easy to get around the 'medicinal' requirement." He smiled.

"My friend's daughter was arrested in Florida while they were on vacation. She was buying ten dollars worth of weed in South Beach. She and her girlfriend were twenty, so they couldn't get into the nightclubs yet. They were looking for something to do. It cost my friend and her husband more than four thousand dollars to get the offense cleared from her record. She wants to be a schoolteacher." I was revving up.

"Obviously that is not okay. We don't do that here," he assured me.

"Even when it's a black guy?" I asked, raising my eyebrows. "You know the statistics."

He laughed and let me go on.

"Sorry. It's a sore subject for me. An adult should be allowed to get a little high when she feels like it. And why are so many young black males in prison for drugs? Honestly, I don't get why the government is so against it. How many people are in the morgue for marijuana overdoses? None! We could stop the drug wars in Mexico if we just legalized it and ran a homegrown campaign. Think of the tax revenue...sorry." I was getting too worked up.

He watched me talk with a slight smile, and I wondered if he'd heard a thing I'd said. I was a little embarrassed and looked away.

"I'd better go pay my respects," he said, interrupting the awkward moment.

"Try not to arrest anyone!" I shouted after him.

I wasn't sure if it was the heat or my banter that had chased him off, nor was I sure if I was relieved or disappointed that he was gone. I had admired plenty of men since Jack, but this was the first one who made my blood rush hot.

Diane showed up moments later, all children's-partied up in a striped green and blue dress and a circus birthday hat.

"It's all I had," she said, obviously self-conscious.

"Do you know the book *Go, Dog. Go!*?" I asked her.

"Of course I do," she answered. "Why?"

"Just wondering," I said, finishing my drink and looking to see where Jason was so I could get another. Alice and I were both drinking Manhattans since they were Martha's favorite.

Diane seemed a bit more confident than I'd seen her in the past. Maybe throwing Wally out had empowered her. He spotted his wife immediately and made his way down the bar. I held out my glass, but he ignored it and leaned over toward Diane.

"I'm so glad you're here," he said softly.

"I wouldn't miss it. You know how much I loved Martha."

"Who has Tabitha?"

"My mom's keeping her overnight."

"I miss her so much."

"Come by and see her tomorrow. Maybe you can take her to the park or something."

Wally's face lit up at the prospect of seeing his daughter. He was behaving remarkably well tonight.

Keep it up, Wally, and soon you'll be a real boy, I thought.

Myles and Sophie came in at eight o'clock. Sophie looked gorgeous in a fuchsia-colored dress, slinky and tight fitting on her curvy frame. Myles wore a nicely tailored gray suit with a pink tie. They both donned shiny silver hats with fringe on their well-coiffed heads.

The pair stuck together out of necessity. Elliot was not speaking to Sophie because she went back to Myles, Sam had never been part of her entourage, and Dan was working at the hospital. She started pawing at Francis Rogers later, talking with her suddenly strong Southern accent. Although I was still sitting right next to him, she didn't acknowledge me. Myles said hello but sensed my disdain and stood back with his hands in his pockets. I saw them leave shortly after nine without saying good-bye.

It was a quietly festive night. The ceiling of the bar twinkled like the night sky, and the lanterns added to the feeling that we were in a tent or a garden. Martha stood watch on her throne, as proud as a jar of ashes could be of a beautiful party. I held my new drink up and toasted her. A full celebration of her life was in progress, just as she had commanded.

At 9:14 p.m., two older men, all tweed and turtleneck, came into the bar. They greeted Francis, and he introduced them as Gregory McClure and Lawrence Ferlinghetti. I couldn't believe I was face-to-face with those two legends of literature and stumbled like an ass on my own words before I finally said, "Nice to meet you." The bar was becoming crowded with the young and old, a former mayor, restaurant owners, and other people I suspected were the somebodies of old San Francisco. I met a waiter from Perry's. He'd been serving her for thirty years. He shed a tear when he told me about the first time they'd met on his first day of work and how he'd screwed up her order and she'd insisted on eating it anyway.

At nine thirty, Dan showed up. He had on a straw hat, the kind you'd wear when campaigning, and a royal-blue polo with wrinkled khakis. He looked around the room like his mother had dropped him off on the first day of school. I felt a little sorry for him. He was an uptight nerd in love with a manipulative woman who was way out of his league. I wondered about my sudden sympathy and chalked it up to his choice of shoes that evening—loafers.

"Come and have a drink with me, Dan." I waved him over, and he smiled with relief. I introduced him to Francis Rogers, who, after ranting about Sophie's figure, was now telling me stories about drinking Bloody Marys with Herb Caen. He took a breath to shake Dan's hand and then started telling midcentury North Beach tales to the lonely doctor.

It took some finagling to make my way down the narrow bar to the restroom. When I walked by Erik, he stood erect to let me pass, but for a moment we were closely face-to-face in the tight space. I looked up at him, and he down at me, and I knew it wasn't just me feeling hot. I may have forgotten to move.

Alice grabbed my arm and led me toward the end of the bar. "Elliot thinks someone pushed him," she whispered.

"What? We were there. No one pushed him." I was looking down the bar at Erik, who was also watching me.

"From down below. He thinks they knocked him off balance. Hey! I'm talking to you." She waved her hand in front of my face, bringing me into the conversation.

"All of my focus was on Elliot's angry face, not the ladder. Why would anyone want to hurt Elliot?" I asked.

"Let's see, Martha plans to evict the Princess unless she leaves Myles, and then Martha ends up dead. Elliot demands she leave Myles, and then he ends up falling from a ladder..."

"Myles!" I said before she could finish. "We know he's violent. But who is going to kill someone in broad daylight while the police are in the building?"

"What better way than to make it look like an accident? Plus, who's to say he knew the cops were there."

"You told Martha about the fighting. You could be next!" I was freaked at the thought.

Alice shrugged, unfazed. "I will kick his ass out of the bay and into the hull of his next ship."

"Don't mess with Alice," I said in a low voice, like an announcer from a monster truck commercial.

At ten o'clock, Wally turned the music down to get our attention. There weren't many of us left: a few people from the neighborhood and the Alder residents, with the exception of Myles and Sophie. Wally had stayed surprisingly sober, and when he spoke up, he was clear and precise.

Erik already knew the contents of the will. I suspected that his real reason for being there had more to do with the observation of the Alder residents and their reactions to the document. For now, he stayed leaning against the wall, and I knew if I wanted to get back to my spot by the door, I would have to brush past him again, which made me schoolgirl happy.

"If you knew my aunt Martha, then it won't come as a surprise to you that she planned her own party tonight. We had strict instructions on how to decorate the room, and as always, she was right; the bar looks great, don't you think?" There was light applause, and he continued. "She loved a good party pretty much more than anything. When I look around the room tonight at the bright colors and the fun hats, I think she would be very happy." His eyes welled up and he took a deep breath. "In her usual fashion, she wanted to do things in an unusual way, so I am going to introduce you to Sally Alan, Aunt Martha's attorney."

I saw Elliot look to Sam, who shrugged in surprise. Sally was a small, thick woman with a Roman nose and a Brooklyn accent that years in San Francisco couldn't shake. I had to smile as she flipped through some papers, looking quite professional with the exception of a bright red fez with a long black tassel dangling from her closely cropped head.

She spoke up in a masculine voice: "Martha Byrne has requested the reading of her last will and testament." She cleared her throat and continued with the formalities that such a document requires, then got down to the details.

"To my nephew Wally McCourt," Sally read, "I leave the Jupiter Bar, a Byrne family business that he has run very successfully."

Wally smiled in what seemed like relief. Elliot, on the other hand, could not hide the anger and disappointment of the announcement. I knew he wasn't a fan of Wally's, but why the emotional investment in the bar? I wondered. I glanced in Erik's direction and saw that he was watching Elliot.

"My property at Twenty Alder Street will be donated to the Bay Area Lesbian, Gay, Bisexual, and Transgender Union, a nonprofit that I have had the honor of supporting for many years. Any tenant that is present at this reading will have a life tenancy in their apartment. Those that are not must vacate within sixty days. Rent is to be paid directly to the trust set up for the organization and must not be increased during the tenancy. Sam Larkin is to act as administrator for the trust and landlord. My apartment is to be leased, rent free, to my nephew Wally McCourt, if he chooses to lease it. All other vacant apartments will be rented in the usual manner at market value."

Wow, free rent for life. Way to go, Martha, I thought.

"My art and jewelry collection is to be auctioned off, with all proceeds going to Malaria Fighters International." I heard my sister gasp in surprise. She leaned on Jason, tears flowing.

"The only exception to the collection will be the portrait of me, by Jean Claude Beaudin, which I leave to my dear friend Alice Harding."

My sister's mouth was agape. I wondered what the painting would be worth at auction—millions was my guess.

"All cash and stocks will be kept in a trust for Tabitha McCourt and any other heirs of my nephew Wally McCourt, upon which time they will be used to pay for college and as a stipend if they choose to live in Paris for one year. I would like it to be known to them that this was my wish. If they choose not to use the stipend, it will be donated to the American Heart Association," Sally read, then looked up from the papers. "This concludes the reading of the last will and testament of Martha Swanson Byrne."

What a lovely and generous woman Martha was! I wished for the hundredth time that week that I could have known her better. My thoughts went back to the evening of her party—Sophie trying to leave early, looking for more fun than an old lady's birthday party could provide her. Martha knew exactly who Sophie was, and her actions had sealed their eviction.

The bar cleared out with the exception of the Alder residents. Erik Healy had slipped out. I felt slighted and relieved at the same time. He was awakening things in me that I hadn't felt in years. It was bad.

Elliot sat alone quietly, no congratulations offered. I wandered over and sat next to him.

"Are you okay?" I asked.

"Sure, sure. I'm fine. Slight headache still, but fine." He wasn't quite slurring, but you could tell by his speech he was drunk. "He had a fat tongue," Alice would have said.

"Alice told me you think someone pushed your ladder?"

"I am sure of it. I have this flash of memory, where I am up there, right, and then the ladder is just gone. Yanked. Gone. You saw it happen, right?"

"Well, kind of. We were upstairs and I was facing you, but I didn't see anything but the fall really. It looked like you lost your balance."

"Oh."

"Why would someone want to hurt you, Elliot?"

"Why would someone kill Martha? I think it's Myles. I really do. He was glaring at me tonight, like he knew that I knew what he had done."

I had missed that and wondered if Elliot was being a little dramatic. The only look I saw on Myles's face was discomfort, but he'd been standing behind me, and I hadn't watched him all night. We were all feeling a little paranoid though. A murderer was among us—there was no forgetting it.

"If Myles killed Martha because he knew about the ultimatum she had given Sophie, and then he tried to kill you because you encouraged her to leave, my sister could be next," I said. "I meant to talk to Erik Healy about this. The will was read and I forgot. I am really worried for her safety."

"If Myles did this, he hates women more than you could know."

"It was that bad?"

"It was worse than you can imagine. There was some rage there, Lee. She was propped up. Sitting up." He was slurring now and still sipping his red wine. I knew he shouldn't be giving me the details, but I had to know.

"She had her kimono on still, but it was open. Wide open. I mean, you could see it all. And her tongue was hanging out, and her hands were behind her back. And the worst part, he stuck a can of PermaNet up her, like fucking Ted Bundy. And her eyes were open and she was looking so dead. She looked really dead," he said. I could see why he'd want to be drunk. I wanted another drink just hearing it.

I was familiar with Ted Bundy's work. He had done the same gruesome thing with a can of hair spray to one of his last victims, a college girl in her dorm room. I wondered if this was a copycat. It hardly seemed likely to me that such an act could happen twice without the second offender knowing about it.

"Eww!" I said. I could see her lying there, under the portrait I had stood under on that very same day. Whoever did this really hated her. Deeply. It was true; Myles was the most likely candidate. He had to have found out somehow about the ultimatum she had given Sophie. Who else would be so angry with Martha?

When we got back to the apartment, I was completely creeped out, double-checking the lock and reminding Jason fifteen times that Alice was in danger.

"Lee, I've got it, okay? Look, here is my baseball bat. No one comes near her without getting this." He swung the bat and made a cracking sound.

"That's Alice's bat."

A call to Erik Healy would be first on my list tomorrow.

I lay in bed watching the shadows of the trees again, thinking of the thick industrial glass that separated me from a violent killer—just a piece of glass. The old industrial windows were made with wire mesh security glass; it would take more than a hammer to break them. I thought of my windows at home—thin in comparison—and yet I'd felt so secure there.

CHAPTER 13

THE EARLY SUN WAS COMING through the front window, warming a spot on the pillow next to me. There seemed to be an ax stuck in my temple, or it felt like it. I mumbled a curse to myself for having that last drink. Still half-asleep, I grabbed at the ringing phone.

"Sorry to wake you, but I was worried. Come home to us." It was my husband, Jack, calling.

"It won't be long now. We're going to Memorial Park tonight. It's going to be so nice to get out of here."

I could barely contain myself. Memorial was home to the coastal redwoods. It was where ferns rose out of the ground in lacy celebration, and chartreuse moss clung to surfaces both natural and manmade, making them glow even on the darkest days. I'd always told my kids that it was where the fairies lived.

"I need to smell some redwoods," I said, practically crawling toward the sink to refill my water glass.

"I'm jealous," he said.

"You just get back to work so I can enjoy these trips," I joked. "And make sure the house is clean when I get back."

"Very funny...your boys miss you. So do the furry ones."

He wasn't trying to make me feel bad, but the words still had that effect. I missed him too, and the ache in my heart for my kids was even worse. But it would be no time at all before I was home again, longing for here. I made the decision to keep my mind in the Bay Area and enjoy every second of it.

"My time here is critical. I need it." I tried to be nice but felt a little impatient with him. Maybe it was the hangover, maybe it was the early call, maybe both.

"Try not to get killed in the process, please?"

I told him I had to go. As soon as I hung up, I dialed Erik.

"Sorry to call so early. I'm really worried about my sister. If my theory is correct, she could be in trouble."

"I'm just leaving the gym. Wanna meet me for coffee?"

"Um..." I was thinking of having this conversation in bed, in my pajamas, but the thought of a hot cup of coffee motivated me, and I knew the fresh air would do me good. "Okay," I answered, kind of excited at the thought of seeing him again.

"Do you know the café at the Flower Mart?"

"Yes, of course." This made me a bit defensive because he obviously didn't see me as a local. I wondered if I was still a local and had my own doubts.

"See you there in twenty minutes."

I threw on a pair of jeans and a T-shirt and tied my hair back in a ponytail. My eyes were bloodshot from the hangover, so I applied mascara and lip gloss, which seemed to only highlight the damage. The crisp morning sun was mood-altering. The air smelled like ocean, and I stopped to take a conscious breath when I reached the corner.

The Flower Mart wasn't far, just down a few blocks of warehouse-lined streets. I arrived in moments. The café sat in the back of the market. Morning light glowed through the stalls, which were speckled with shopkeepers picking up last-minute orders. Flowers of every kind were stuffed in rows of white buckets making an urban field of color. Fresh-cut greens and roses, lilies, and lilacs tossed their scent around in competition, and I entered the restaurant feeling slightly better.

The café was more like a diner you'd see in Jersey, with dated booths and Formica tables. It hadn't changed since the last time I was here, which was probably two decades ago. I wondered how long it would be before it was gone. Erik was seated at a table, showered and dressed in a black fleece zip-up, a white T-shirt, and jeans. His salt-and-pepper hair was slightly messy in a look that said, "day off." I liked casual Erik.

"Good morning," I said, feeling suddenly shy.

"How are you?" he asked with a knowing smile.

"It's like there is an arrow through my head." I winced.

"Did you take something?"

"I'm allergic to anything worth taking. Long story...but it's why I started smoking weed." I didn't want to have that conversation, so I followed it with, "Anyway..." The truth was that I couldn't wait to smoke when I got back to Alice's; it would cure the nausea and headache faster than a caramel.

"What's going on?" he asked after the waitress brought me coffee.

"You're aware of the situation with Myles and Sophie, right?"

"That he pushes her around?"

"Yeah, that," I said with a look of distaste. "Elliot thinks the fall wasn't an accident. He thinks someone grabbed the ladder from below."

He sat silently for a moment. I expected an objection based on the fact that he was a witness to the fall, but he didn't say a word.

"Why would someone want to do that to Elliot?" he asked.

"His fall was the morning after the big blowout with Myles. Sophie spent the night with Elliot and Sam, but in the morning she snuck back up to Myles and they 'made up.'" I emphasized the last part, thinking of the racket they made that morning. It wasn't the loud makeup sex—although I couldn't help thinking they knew we could hear them—but the nature of the fight itself. I found them sadistic, and the look on my face portrayed my feelings.

Erik laughed and waited for me to continue.

"Elliot is really pissed off at Sophie for going back. He thinks Myles killed Martha because she gave Sophie an ultimatum, and he thinks Myles came after him for the same reason. Myles is an angry guy."

"Angry enough to try to kill someone in broad daylight?"

"Elliot got way too drunk last night and told me how he found Martha. It's horrible. Whoever did this had a major grudge against women. Doesn't Myles fit the profile?"

"It's not impossible, but we have no proof. The apartment search produced nothing to lead us to believe he was involved."

"What were you looking for that day in the apartments? Can you say?"

He laughed a little at my tenacity and then told me. I couldn't believe it, but he did.

"We didn't find any fingerprints on her body. We suspect the assailant used gloves, maybe a bag to suffocate her. Also, her jade necklace is missing, the one she wore the evening of her homicide. I really shouldn't be telling you this. I'm trusting you to keep that to yourself, please."

I wished I hadn't asked. "Of course. But why? Why not just strangle her?"

"Who knows? The bag would prevent any transfer of DNA to the murderer, so it was smart on the part of the killer...and it was taken with him."

I noticed that he said "him" and wondered if it was an accident. They say women prefer poison, which just proves we are the more civilized sex, but a young woman could overpower a person of Martha's age. It wasn't impossible.

"But wouldn't she struggle to rip it off?"

"She was restrained with the belt of her kimono. According to the medical examiner, she didn't put up much of a fight. There wasn't much bruising around her wrists. We haven't located the gloves or a bag. They're probably in the city sewer system at this point."

"So this was well planned. Doesn't seem like Myles's style. What about the Princess? She's cunning." Even as I said it, I knew it couldn't be her. She wouldn't dirty up her hands like that.

"She has a solid alibi—dancing on the bar for most of the night." He smiled at my comment, knowing exactly whom I meant.

I thought back to that evening. What he said was true—nothing was going to pry Sophie from the limelight that night. Her desire for attention had created a perfect alibi.

"So, who does that leave...Dr. Dan, but he was at the bar all night too, eyes glued to Sophie. Did you check to see if he was there all night?"

He rolled his eyes.

"Okay. Wally is cleared. There's Jason, but he doesn't have the motive or the anger, plus he was with me in the apartment. I'm his alibi. And my sister..."

He was waiting for me, five steps ahead of my thoughts, but I kept at it.

"Does Myles have a solid alibi?"

He nodded.

"So Sam is the only one who returned to his apartment alone. Sam is the only one without a solid alibi?" There was no way I could believe Sam was capable of such a thing. "No way. No way...he would not hurt Elliot. Why would he hurt Elliot? Or Martha for that matter?"

He sat patiently while I rolled through the logic, allowing me to catch up.

"He was downstairs when Elliot fell," I said slowly. "But what would his motive be for killing Martha?" I gasped. "Do you think he knew about the will? But who kills someone over foundation money? It's not like she left it to him! No way. He didn't do this," I finally finished.

"Look, Lee, this is all speculation. We still don't even know if someone broke into the place. We're still checking on former tenants, local robberies, interviewing witnesses..."

"Former tenants. I didn't think of that. But my sister is the newest tenant there. Those apartments have been rented for years. Why would a former tenant kill her now?"

I didn't expect an answer. I knew they had to check out all the angles.

"If Myles didn't do it, it has to be Dan," I said.

"What motive would Dan have for killing Martha?"

"Maybe he didn't want Sophie to go. He's in love with her, you know. What's up with men anyway? Any woman could see in two seconds that she is not exactly a quality human."

"It's not her quality as a human that attracts men." He smiled.

"You too?" I rolled my eyes.

"No, no. I could see right through that. Not my type." He looked away from me when he said that last sentence.

There was a moment of silence as I wondered if I was his type. Then I remembered that it looked like I had gravel in my eyes. "Okay, I have to go. We're getting out of the murder bunker to go camping," I said, scooting out of the booth.

"Enjoy. We're supposed to have a couple of beautiful days."

"You didn't say good-bye last night."

He looked up at me but didn't say a word. I walked away before he could think of a reply.

Play with fire much? I asked myself on the way back. I pushed him out of my mind and went back to the situation at Alder. I had Sam on my mind. There was something bothering me, something that I had to figure out. I was in deep thought when I passed the Jupiter. The door was open, and I couldn't see inside the bar because of the light.

"Lee!"

"Hey, Wally. What are you doing here so early?"

He came out of the bar to greet me, holding a broom in his hand. His hair was a mess as usual, but he looked better than I felt.

"Just cleaning up from last night. I didn't have a single drink at the wake. I'm amazed at how good I feel today."

"Good for you! Hey, I have a question for you. Do you know what happened to your uncle Harry's ex-wife, Jane?"

His forehead wrinkled for a moment and he looked up, like the sky had the answer.

"Yeah, my mom was good friends with her for years. Mom moved up to Portland after Harry divorced. It was pretty heartbreaking for her. She never forgave Harry, and she never really liked Martha for it. She was Catholic, and you just didn't get a divorce back then. My dad cheated on her, I found out later, but he never left, and I think that was somehow more noble to her."

I guessed that had been where he'd learned his bad husband behaviors.

"What about their baby?" I asked.

"She didn't have any kids with Harry."

"Is Jane still alive?" I asked.

"No. She was sick with cancer at around the same time my mom was. She died first. What's with all the interest?"

"I just find Martha's life interesting," I said. "My sisters and I are going camping tonight. It's going to be good to get away for a bit."

"Yeah. Not exactly a cheerful place, is it?" His voice reflected the recent tragedy. I gave him a rub on the shoulder and a sympathetic smile, and he soaked it up like a neglected puppy.

"Have a great time. See you on the water on Sunday?"

Jason was right; Wally could be sweet. I had no reason to be there on Sunday. It was an intimate moment for Martha's family and friends, and yet he was generous enough to include me like family.

"You won't mind if I'm there?" I asked.

"Of course not. You're Jason and Alice's family, so you're my family." He smiled.

Martha had left instructions for them to take the dragon jar out to the Golden Gate and release her ashes. It's illegal to dump ashes into the bay, but the captain was an old friend of Martha's and agreed to respect her request. She was very specific about being dropped at the Golden Gate, which is the opening from the San Francisco Bay to the Pacific Ocean. The water was rough out there, and I usually got very seasick—unless I was high. I would be eating a caramel that day, appropriate or not; it was truly medicinal this time.

When I entered the courtyard, I could hear signs of life for the first time in days. Dishes clattered and someone was listening to KFOG. I heard the familiar voice of my favorite DJ.

Ahh, home, I thought.

If San Francisco could talk, it would sound like Dave Morey's gentle voice. He spoke to us like a favorite uncle, never unkind, and always knowing what we needed to hear. We had great pride in our local musicians in the Bay Area, and Morey was the guy who brought them to us. Talk of his retirement brought sadness to my heart. I wondered how the station would make it without him.

Morey played Carlos Santana's "Europa (Earth's Cry Heaven's Smile)." The instrumental song held in it all the passion and beauty of the city and reminded me of the day Jerry Garcia died. It was played in tribute as San Francisco mourned the loss of a brother. I stopped short to listen, then realized it was coming from Alice and Jay's and started up the stairs.

"Lee!" I heard before I made it two steps.

It was Elliot, looking clammy and gray.

"Yikes!"

"I never drink like that. I guess it was all just getting to me," he said.

"It's a lot for me too, and I hardly knew Martha. I can only imagine what it's like for you, being so close to her and all. And having to live with the Ted Bundy thing! Shit."

His faced changed to a bright red. "You know about that?"

"Sorry, you spilled it last night. I don't want to share that vision with anyone, trust me. I won't say a word."

He just stood there, blank. It made me uncomfortable.

"Gotta go," I said. "We're going camping for a few days. I need the smell of redwoods, and definitely need to hit Duarte's for some artichoke and green chili soup...sourdough, olallieberry pie...I really do eat my way across the state when I come here." I was rambling uncomfortably upstairs to the door, not sure he could even hear my words.

"Hey, sistah!" Alice yelled from the bedroom when I came in. "You better pack it up. Lacy will be here any minute."

I sat down on the couch and lit up a joint, feeling the ease of its effects wash over me like a warm wave of peace, instantly free of reality's burdens.

CHAPTER 14

THE PACIFIC COAST HIGHWAY, OR Highway 1, as we referred to it in Northern California, snaked along the water, winded around bays, and then dropped into perfect views of the wild Pacific. Its habits, colors, and sea life were as familiar to me as my family's history. I'd bobbed in its freezing waters, peered down at seaweed forests, waded through rocky tide pools, and stood on the shore while whales playfully breached in its deep breaks.

Our father loved the ocean and brought us to the beach every chance he got. He bought me my first wetsuit when I was ten years old—you need one to swim in the chilly waters of the north Pacific. "Never turn your back on the ocean." I remembered the words but couldn't hear his voice anymore. He always brought an empty garbage bag, and we'd leave the beach with a sack full of litter. "Do you want a sea turtle eating that?" he would say if we resisted. "It's our job to protect them from us humans." My father would be appalled by the new world of plastic water bottles and disposable containers.

A long day on the beach always ended with a bonfire. The four of us would huddle around with blankets while Dad night fished for smelt. We would drive home with sandy feet and fish scales on our hands and a warm layer of color. The sadness returned when I thought of our family intact. I wondered if the cancer had already been working at its evil mission to steal my childhood, faith, and security.

"The fog is as reliable as the Kennedy curse," I said as we drove through the north side of Pacifica, or P-Town, as the locals called it. I'd once dated a guy from the dreary town. Their street fair was appropriately called the Fog Fest. Floats with freezing mermaids would idle down the main street, the shells on their breasts hiding the cold from the bundled audience of children.

The wet air broke in perfect time to reveal my first view of the Pacific, undisturbed with the exception of the rocky Farallon Islands jutting into shark-infested ice water. The fact that we could see them was a predictor of how good the weather was going to be.

We were in Lacy's convertible Audi, the top was down, and loose hair was escaping from my ponytail, slapping me rhythmically and stinging my face. An Indigo Girls CD was blaring, and we were singing along with enormous smiles. "Closer to Fine" was our anthem. I was never safer than when I was with these women who knew me so well and loved me so deeply.

My normal concerns about other people's driving didn't apply today. Lacy had never been in an accident or gotten a speeding ticket, or even locked her keys in the car for that matter. As the only adult in the family, she couldn't afford to. I didn't have to hold onto the strap for safety or white knuckle the dash as I did with every other driver I knew. We cruised over Devil's Slide, a winding two-lane road that didn't allow for error. I was able to peek down at the steep, sheer cliffs and enjoy the white-capped waters below without fear.

We drove past WWII bunkers which were built to spot the Japanese but were now becoming one with their bluffs as the earth around them wandered into the sea. I scanned the horizon for migrating gray whales but didn't see any telltale white spouts. We passed gull-filled harbors and small coastal villages. A flock of pelicans flew overhead as we hit the open farmlands where the cliffs ended abruptly at the rough water.

When I was a kid, a cow fell to its death from the cliffs above one of our family's favorite spots, Martin's Beach. It was legend now. "Remember the cow?" friends at the beach would ask. I could tell a story about every one of the beaches that we drove past that day: we'd once paid a farmer for access to a cove that we could only get down to by climbing a rope, there was a beach that was full of pebbles, and another one was where Alice buried Lacy's jacket and never found it. My mother was so angry. We dug holes all over the beach looking for it that day.

A left turn at an artichoke stand brought us to a snakelike country road, and we arrived at Duarte's Tavern just in time for lunch. We waited for our table in the ancient dark bar that our grandfather used to frequent—he'd lived less than a mile away. This was a place of legacy for our family. I wondered if he'd sat in my seat and what they'd talked about there in the midst of the fields.

After lunch, we picked up a fresh-baked flat of artichoke focaccia and two bottles of red wine and set off through the winding narrow road that was shaded by redwoods and hugged the creek that fed the ancient giants. The air smelled of their woodsy majesty.

The Hardings were tree huggers, there was no shame in admitting it, and we got the best hug out of the velvety bark of a redwood tree. They were so ancient that Jesus shared the same time period with them, and they were magnificently large enough to remind you of your insignificance. I would be hugging more than a few on that day.

Shrubby laurel and swords of lacy fern sprung from the forest floor. The occasional clearing revealed a blackberry-covered fence with a nestled cabin. Lacy turned into the park and pulled past the ranger station into a temporary space. The sunlight streamed through the treetops, creating warm spotlights through the towering giants. We approached the booth to register for a site and chitchat about the park as we always had.

"Hello, ladies. Spending the day with us today?" We didn't look like campers in the clean white convertible, which was hardly over-flowing with equipment.

"Hello, sir," said Lacy. "We're actually spending the night. Or we'd like to. Do you have any sites available?"

"Yes, ma'am, we do." He laughed. "I hope you brought your jack-ets and winter bags. It's still pretty chilly here at night."

"Chilly." I laughed. *None of you know what chilly is*, I thought.

"Don't worry about us, Larry. We've been at this for years," Alice told him.

"Well, the park is pretty quiet this time of year—just a day camp-er or two. Where would you like to be?"

He showed us the map, and we picked a spot we'd camped in be-fore. It was close to the creek and also close to the restrooms, but not too close. Camping with us wasn't like real camping—yes, we slept on the ground in a tent, but meals were eaten out, the only camping utensil we brought was a wine opener, and the only equipment packed were some flashlights and a lantern. Breakfast was fetched from the same little market where we bought our firewood—egg sandwiches made by a woman at that same market, who may or may not have realized she'd known us our entire lives. The point was to relax, and we had it down.

As soon as we pulled up, Alice and I wandered off. Lacy yelled at us to help her set up the tent.

"Look, we're right by a fairy ring," Alice said. I wandered over to look but, on my way, heard her say, "Uh-oh."

A circle of ashy white dust and what looked like tiny broken sea-shells were scattered in a ring inside the circle of trees. Redwoods did best when they sprouted around the base of an existing tree. When the mother tree died, they would feed off her root system and grow up around her, creating sheltered circles in the forest, their roots connecting underground to keep them stronger in storms. In their center, they would have a soft red carpet. When we were kids, we made forts in them, pretending to be woodland creatures. We'd spread blankets on the cushion of ground and stare up in awe at the treetops, which seemed to touch the heavens. It was obvious that someone found the ring as magical as we did and had chosen to scatter a loved one's remains there.

"I didn't know ashes were so chunky," Alice said.

"Yeah, I kind of figured we'd be dust." I could see little bone fragments, and the metal tag from the funeral home had been left behind. It was close to our campsite and disturbed me for a moment, but thinking of the way the family had obeyed their loved one's wishes made it feel more sacred than macabre.

We decided not to tell Lacy, as she might want to move to another campsite, and neither of us wanted that. She yelled again for us to help and we joined her. The tent was new and had bendable poles. We popped it up in minutes.

"Remember that musty old circus tent Mom and Dad had? Whatever happened to that?" I asked.

"I got rid of it when we sold the house," Lacy said. "It was covered in mildew and spiders."

I could still smell the musty air inside the tent. It was huge. Or was I just small? My father would turn into a cranky beast while he set it up. Lacy was just like him. I walked over and gave her a hug.

"Love you, little sister," she whispered.

"Thanks for taking care of us," I whispered back.

There was a creek-side trail a few steps from our site. We headed down it to our favorite crescent-moon sliver of beach where the water was deep enough to fish and swim but bitter cold. The roots of a large tree were exposed in the bank and searched their way into the creek like tentacles—ferns took the opportunity to nestle into the spaces in between. The light was shining onto the beach through the surrounding trees, creating a cathedral-like effect. In the sacred space we quietly separated, with Lacy reading a book in the shade and Alice reading her work e-mails on her phone. I'd brought *A Moveable Feast* with me and was flat out on my back, starring up at the breathtakingly high treetops until I almost started to doze.

For someone who was incredibly paranoid about wild animals, Memorial Park was a dream—no bears, snakes, or predatory animals. I could relax without worrying about being eaten. I had always been sensitive to the presence of others and felt like someone or something was with us. I looked up the embankment. In the trees above the small ravine was a figure in a baseball cap—and he seemed to be watching us. In a flash he was gone.

Day hiker, I thought. *Or pervert.*

"Did you see that guy?"

"It's a park, Lee," Alice said without looking up from her BlackBerry. Both of my sisters were well accustomed to my paranoia.

Later, we hiked along the creek-side trail, which rose and fell from the water at different points. An aging suspension bridge spanned the creek, and Alice ran to the center and rocked it back and forth.

"I'm not stepping foot on that thing," I said. "Remember when you left me in the middle of it when we were kids?"

"Poor Lee. We really tortured you," Alice said.

"You mean *you* tortured me."

She was the one who made it rock and sway while I held on for dear life. Lacy had demanded that she stop. When she finally did, I was in tears.

"It's no wonder that I'm afraid of heights."

We stopped at a hollow fallen tree that we had played on as kids. We could have walked hunchbacked through the inside if we didn't mind spiderwebs. Instead, we sat on top, reading the carved names of the past and reminiscing about previous stays.

"No one on the East Coast believed that trees could get so big, so they actually removed the bark of a redwood and reassembled it at the World's Fair so people could see it. The poor tree died from exposure, and people still thought it was a hoax," I told them.

"Your trees are super skinny out there," Alice replied.

"My trees?" I laughed. The aspen, birch, and hemlock forests of the East Coast were spectacular in their own way. "You can't beat the colors in the fall though."

"Skinny," Alice replied. Neither of my sisters could stand for me to say anything nice about my life there. To them, it was my captor.

We still hadn't seen a soul. I mentioned the figure on the cliff again, but my sisters shrugged it off. With the exception of a small white Gocar in the day-users lot, it appeared we had the park to ourselves.

After sharing a bottle of wine at our camp, we headed back to Duarte's for dinner. We ordered the exact same meal we'd had at lunch. Duarte's green chili and artichoke soup—regulars knew that mixing the two soups made one of the best meals on the planet. I'd tried to replicate it, but it was never as good as the real thing.

"I would swim in it if I could," Alice said.

It's true, it was amazing soup, but being stoned enhanced the flavors, and we were both ecstatic.

Lacy did a lot of eye rolling, but when we returned to the park, she asked Alice for a caramel.

"If I have to listen to you dumb shits giggle all night, I may as well be there with you."

"But, Lacy, what if you get addicted? It's a gateway drug, you know," I jabbed.

"Brat," she replied.

The campsite was dark. The giant trees kept the moon out completely. Lacy started a fire in the old stone pit, and I grabbed a bag of chips from the back of the car and threw them on the picnic table. At that point, we were pretty high, wandering around to get stuff, then forgetting what we were looking for. I was thinking my way through the campsite, my head full of abandoned thoughts of brilliance, when I noticed a large fluffy animal ripping at my chips.

"Raccoon!" I shouted. The masked bandit grabbed the bag and ran out of the camp. Lacy had a flashlight.

"Get him!" she shouted and charged after him in the dark.

I watched a bouncing light running after the sound of chips rustling through the woods, but I was behind her by some distance, slowed by laughter that was causing me to stop and buckle. Alice was doing slightly better and was halfway between Lacy and me. In the darkness of the forest, I could see the light turn back toward me, giving up the chase. At the same time, something moved toward me from behind, and as I turned to see it, I let out a piercing scream, which the trees echoed as if protecting me.

CHAPTER 15

IN THE BLINDNESS OF THE night forest, a black shadow had emerged behind me. Like earlier in the day, I'd felt him before I'd seen him. The shape of danger in the darkness. I was paralyzed. He too was stopped, from the shock of my scream? It seemed like an eternity, but Alice was by my side in seconds, and as fast as he'd materialized, he was gone. Silent. Disappeared.

"There's a fucking guy out here!" I said. "It's that guy from today."

"Are you sure you're just not paranoid? From the weed maybe?" Lacy asked.

"Yes! He was coming at me!"

"I'm getting my bat," Alice said.

We walked back to camp arguing over what I had seen. We picked up the bat and our phones and headed to the ranger station.

"Maybe he was just walking and you scared the daylights out of him, Lee," Lacy suggested.

"No way. He was following us. He was lurking."

"That little shit stole our chips," Alice said, laughing. But we weren't quite as carefree as we had been before.

"There's a serial killer in the woods," I told the ranger.

My sisters smiled at each other, and the ranger asked me how I knew it was a serial killer.

"He was dressed in dark clothes and following us. He was going to kill me. Who else kills people in the dark woods?" I said, trusting completely the danger that I had felt.

Alice started laughing that buzzed laugh that comes at inappropriate times, like when you are telling the ranger about a real threat. He looked at us suspiciously.

"Seriously, someone was out there," Lacy said with authority. "We are here because our friend was just murdered in the city. We wanted to get away," she complained as if we were at a five-star hotel and found bedbugs.

"Ma'am, there was only one other visitor here today. He stayed long past his day-use hours and left right before you got here," he answered Lacy like she was his supervisor.

"What did he look like?" I asked.

"I didn't really get a good look at him. He was a white guy, with a baseball hat on and a dark jacket and pants. Now that I think of it, he charged out of here pretty fast."

"In the white Gocar?" I asked.

"Yeah, it was the white car that had been here all day."

"What the fuck?" I said out loud but mostly to myself.

"Sorry, she's from the East Coast," Alice apologized.

"Well, he's gone now," Lacy said. "And I will gouge his eyes out if he comes anywhere near us again."

"She's from here," Alice said to the ranger.

I laughed but knew she would do it if the opportunity presented itself.

"You could hang him off a cliff too," I said.

She'd threatened to do just that to an old boyfriend of mine many years ago. We still reminded her of it regularly. The ranger was confused. We laughed hard, the way we did when things got crazy for us. He suggested we move to a site closer to the station, but it was dark, and we were not in the right mind to find our own pajamas, let alone move everything. He walked us back to our campsite.

"It's like you're a murder magnet," Alice said to me.

I wanted to come up with some smart-ass comment but couldn't think of anything.

"A death decoy," I said, settling.

"Poor Lee," she responded sarcastically.

We didn't allow each other any self-pity for long. She poked me with a stick she'd been playing with, and I threw a small branch at her. We went on like this for a few minutes. Lacy was sitting quietly on a folding chair in front of the fire she'd managed to build for us.

"Are you freaking out, Lace?" Alice asked her.

"Yes, I'm freaking out! I'm stoned out of my mind!"

Alice and I looked at each other, then opened another bottle of wine and sat next to her.

"We finally get Lacy to partake, and that guy fucks it up," I said, poking the fire with a stick.

Furry little opportunistic thieves were hanging around camp, their eyes glowing from the light of the fire, but we had secured our food safely in the car. We shouted obscenities at them for stealing our chips. I tried to tell my sisters a story about my kids but forgot what I was talking about halfway through. Lacy was quiet for the rest of the evening, and I felt bad about giving her the caramel—it wasn't for everyone.

Personally, I was grateful for the drugs and alcohol, which aided me in a perfect night's sleep. We took our time packing up the next day. Lacy was exhausted because, while Alice and I crashed hard, she had been flat on her back staring at the tent ceiling, the bat on her chest, listening for the intruder's return.

As tired as she might have been, she wouldn't let either of us drive. We headed north up the coast, stopping wherever we wanted and singing our hearts out to every song we heard on KFOG. We hit a couple of shops on Main Street in Half Moon Bay, where I bought my kids some gifts. The little coastal town was the only stop between San Francisco and Santa Cruz that had a commercial district. It was lined with coffee shops and independent retail stores, and the greatest tack shop on the coast. We popped in to see the baby chicks and rifle through the round rack of flannel shirts.

"That was a Gocar. I saw the sticker—he had to be from the city. Why would a serial killer come all the way from the city to Memorial Park to kill someone?" I asked while we sipped our coffee at some hippie café. Indonesian fabrics swung from the ceiling, and the walls were hand painted with sayings from Gandhi and other peacemakers. A sun-bleached guitar player hummed folk music on a tiny stage only two feet from our table.

"I think the point is to not get caught, Lee. They usually travel."

"Well, he must not have a car of his own. Maybe it was Myles and he came down here to kill you. He thought I was you in the dark," I suggested, knowing it didn't make any sense. Sophie and Myles had a car.

"That guy was there when we got there," Lacy said. "He was trolling for trouble, and we were the only trouble there." She said it in her "that is the end of it" voice, and we all moved on.

Alice commanded the radio on the way home. Dave Morey continued the long-running tradition of playing "Smoke Two Joints"—or "I Spoke to Joyce" as Bay Area parents told their kids—at five p.m. I had forgotten about this tradition, and it occurred to me that maybe my kids were better off being raised on the East Coast. Regardless, the two of us sang, "I spoke to Joyce in the morning, I spoke to Joyce at night, I spoke to Joyce in the afternoon, and it makes me feel all right," with enormous smiles.

Lacy had never heard the song. She didn't listen to KFOG. She didn't think the song was funny.

"I am amazed that they still do that," I told them.

"I am amazed they do it at all. What kind of message does that send to kids?" Lacy asked.

"That Joyce is a good listener," Alice added, and we laughed.

We stopped at our favorite burrito stand for dinner and then headed back over Devil's Slide toward the city. The fog was so thick that we couldn't see the car in front of us. It was chilly with the top down, but the heater was on full blast. Like many return trips, it was silent in the car, no radio, no chatter, as we returned to the sadness and fear of Alder Street.

"I don't want to leave you guys here," Lacy said sadly when we pulled into the alley.

"I don't want you to leave us here," replied Alice.

Erik Healy opened the door to Alder before we could retrieve our bags from the trunk.

"What are you doing here?" asked Alice.

"Good to see you too." He laughed.

"Is everyone alive in there?" she asked.

"Yes. I'm sorry if I startled you. I had to follow up on something with Dan Stockton."

"Oh," Alice said with relief.

"It was a fun trip. Except when we were attacked by a serial killer in the park," I stated calmly.

"What?"

"We don't know that he was a serial killer, and he didn't lay a hand on anyone," Lacy said, rolling her eyes at me.

"Yeah, well, he came at me in the dark, then ran away when I screamed and the others came to my rescue. Another Ted Bundy episode was avoided."

"Ted Bundy?" He looked at me with squinting eyes now, waiting for more.

"Yeah, you know," I said back at him, giving him a "shut up, it's a secret" look.

I hadn't told my sisters about Elliot's story. It was horrific, and I didn't want them to have the same gruesome images in their minds. Even someone as sick-minded as Alice would be brokenhearted to know what happened to her friend. The detective looked stunned. I figured he really didn't know what I was talking about since I wasn't supposed to know what happened that night. But he knew Elliot had drunkenly spilled the story.

The courtyard was filled with residents. It almost felt like nothing had happened. Dan was wearing his fucking clogs again, drinking a beer by the bar with Sam. I looked at Alice and then looked at Dan's feet. She looked away and laughed. *So petty,* I thought, feeling a little bit ashamed. Myles and Sophie had decided to show their faces. I was surprised that the group was back together again. Myles was manning the grill, keeping to himself. Sophie was sitting with Elliot. It occurred to me that this odd mix of people really were more family than friends.

"How was the trip?" asked Sam.

We looked tired and dirty.

"I'd rather have sex with a woman than sleep in the dirt," Elliot said.

Sam rolled his eyes and shook his head, smiling. "I used to do a lot of backpacking before I met Elliot. I like being outdoors," he told us.

"I needed to smell the trees," I said. "You can't imagine how much I miss that smell."

We didn't mention the attack in the park. I looked at Myles to see if he was waiting for us to mention it, but he showed no signs of nervousness.

Lacy wanted her own shower and bed, so we said our good-byes and she left. Alice and I went to her apartment to clean up and joined the others downstairs shortly. Twilight rested on the courtyard, and the magic reappeared, although not as brilliantly as before. The trees were lit, soft music played, and cocktails flowed while Myles grilled dinner and everyone brought out side dishes from their apartments. The group was in sync, and the casual event fell into magazine-worthy splendor with ease. I pictured the photo spread: gorgeous Sophie laughing over something someone said, wineglass in hand with the blurred table behind her; a shot of handsome Jason holding out one of his gourmet platters, garnished perfectly in bright fresh basil. The table was set with an eclectic assortment of Italian ceramics. The title would read, "Living on Alder Street," but the truth was more like "Death on Alder Street."

"I hear you got the Healy treatment, Dan," Alice fished.

He let out a little "Huh!" I guessed that was his laugh. With a dead serious tone, he said, "He wanted to know if I murdered Martha."

"Well, that is the question, isn't it?" Elliot added sarcastically. "Who done it?"

"I told him I came back here that night." It was a statement more than a confession.

We were all quiet for a moment.

"Why didn't you say anything earlier?" Sam asked him.

"No one asked me. Did anyone ask you, Myles?" He glared. I didn't know he had it in him.

"Yes, actually. Someone did ask me," Myles replied snidely.

"Well, I came back here. And Martha was alive and well at the time. I saw her look out the window," Dan said.

"So she was killed after that," Alice said.

More silence. Eventually, people made conversation again. Elliot pulled me aside to tell me again how sorry he was for being so drunk the other night.

"You didn't tell Alice what I told you, did you?"

"God no! I don't want that image in her head. I don't even want it in mine."

"I'm so sorry."

"I asked you, Elliot. I knew you were drunk. I'm the one that should apologize."

"Well, please don't say anything. I would hate to compromise the case because of my big mouth."

"Mum's the word," I assured him.

"Good night, all. I'm exhausted after sleeping in the dirt." Alice smiled at Elliot. She kissed Jason and went upstairs. I followed shortly, saying my good-nights and looking forward to the comfort of the sofa bed and its protruding metal bar.

CHAPTER 16

MY PHONE RANG EARLY, BEFORE I had lifted my head off the pillow but after I had opened my eyes. I sat up quickly when I saw that it was Erik.

"Coffee?"

"This is becoming a habit, Detective Healy," I said while brushing my hair with my fingers as if he could see me. "People will talk."

"Apparently they already are. That's why I want to meet."

"We have Martha's..." I stopped. "We're doing a little memorial service this morning for Martha. Can we meet later?"

"I saw the funeral plans, Lee. I know what you're up to today. It's illegal to dispose of a body within three miles of a shoreline. We wouldn't want her bridgework washing up on Baker Beach, now would we?"

"You wouldn't want to upset a nice dead lady like Martha, would you?" I asked.

"I can't hear you. I don't know a thing," he said. "What about you? Cremated or buried?"

"Buried," I answered. "But in a wicker basket so the worms can get me."

He made a noise indicating I'd grossed him out.

"I don't want to be baked. Or embalmed. Just a nice grassy hill somewhere. My kids can plant a tree on top of me. I'll nourish the tree. What about you?"

"I thought I knew up until about a minute ago." He laughed. "What time can we meet? I really need to talk to you."

"Okay. How about three o'clock? The stands at Aquatic Park? I can walk over there later."

"See you then."

Before I could put much thought into what he wanted, Alice walked into the living room, rubbing her head, and started the coffee-making process.

"What's up, Dummy?" she asked.

"It was Jack," I lied. "He forgot about the time change again. Sorry."

"It's time to get up anyway. I'm really looking forward to getting today over with. Once those ashes are gone, maybe we can return to some normalcy around here."

"Uhh, not really, Al. There is that whole murder thing to resolve."

"Ugh! It's such a nightmare. I just want it to go away."

"Well, if the murderer isn't caught, you're going to live here wondering who it is. Do you really want to live like that?"

Jason wandered into the kitchen.

"Morning, ladies," he spoke softly, but even with a hangover, he had a chipper tone. "Let me do that, hon," he said as he nudged her aside and made coffee. "Go hang with your sis."

"Drink a little last night, Jay?" I teased.

"Hey, guess who showed up again last night?" Jason asked.

We both waited for an answer instead of guessing.

"Officer Fat Head. He's stationed in front of Martha's door again."

"Why?" Alice and I said at the exact same moment.

"Who knows? He wasn't saying, and trust me, we asked."

"We were in that apartment. It's not like we can't get in. What are they protecting?"

Jason just shook his head and shrugged.

"What do you wear to an ash-throwing ceremony?" I asked Alice. She didn't know either. I settled on a simple top and pants. I tossed an orange scarf around my neck for color, thinking of Martha.

We'd rented a van to bring us all to the marina. Wally and Diane were meeting us there with Martha's remains.

"She bought that jar in my shop," Elliot told us on the ride over. "That's how I met her. She came in, with her crazy red hair and some brightly colored pashmina looking for midcentury art books. When she saw the jar, she 'had to have it.' It was a small fortune, but she didn't blink. I looked her up online and found out about her past as a muse and artist. She has a Wiki page, you know?" He didn't wait for an answer. "I started collecting the books for her. One night she showed up while I was closing. We went out for cocktails. I told her we were looking for an apartment. She told me about Alder. At first I said thanks but no thanks. We needed two bedrooms, but she insisted we come see it, and the rest is history."

"Who was going to buy the bar?" I asked him suddenly, surprising myself, as well as the rest of the passengers.

"A client," he answered, visibly put off by the question.

"But how did that come about? Did she tell you she wanted to sell the bar?"

"Jesus, what do you care?" sneered Sophie.

I ignored her completely.

"Do not talk to my sister like that, Sophie." Alice was giving her the Harding evil eye.

"Don't, Alice. It's fine," I said.

I'd seen Alice get mad on my behalf before. It was not pretty, and Sophie was smart enough to sense it and shut her highly glossed mouth.

"It was a great opportunity," Elliot said. "When he told me he was looking for new properties, I told him about the Jupiter. Martha wasn't getting any younger, and I thought she was mad at Wally. I didn't know she'd leave him the bar. I still can't believe she did. That will must have been very old."

It was a great opportunity for you, I thought, wondering what his finder's fee was.

"It was three weeks old, Elliot," Alice chimed in.

He was having a hard time hiding his disgust.

"Wally's a good guy. You should give him a chance," Alice added.

Elliot was particularly pissy today, but he folded his arms and kept quiet.

The green was alive with kites sailing, kids running, and couples holding hands along the water. The Marina Yacht Club is one of only a few complexes on this northern span of water. Behind it sits the remnants of the 1915 World's Fair, the Palace of Fine Arts, with its graceful rotunda and grand colonnades. The structure was built with wooden foundations and plaster forms. It was never supposed to survive the wet air and rumbling earth. But San Franciscans fell in love with the romance of the palace. It was constantly being restored and was considered a permanent part of the city's character.

From the northern-facing windows of the yacht club, the bridge and headlands created a breathtaking view. The docks were lined with old-money water toys. Captain George Sloan greeted us at one of them, a thirty-foot weekender moored along the dock with several other fine vessels. Wally and Diane followed closely behind us, dragon jar in hand.

"You're supposed to conceal that, friend. I can get in big trouble," mumbled the captain.

"I'm sorry," said Wally. "We were running late and I forgot."

He took the jar down below for safekeeping, and we left the harbor, heading toward the bridge.

It was a beautiful day on the water, but even the most beautiful day under the Golden Gate was rough. I had expected to be queasy, so I had taken half of a caramel for seasickness. If there was one great thing about weed, it was that it was a miraculous cure for nausea. I felt justified for being high on such an occasion. It was certainly better than barfing on Martha's watery grave.

See…medicinal, I thought to Erik Healy, as if he could read my mind.

Wally was asked to do the honors, and the captain looked the other way while we gathered together for a few words. You could hear the cars crossing the grates on the bridge above us. Fort Point, the old Civil War encampment that once protected the bay, sat quietly on our left, while the Marin Headlands waited for us across the water.

Everyone was asked to talk about a favorite memory with Martha. Dan told a story about how he had met her. He was just out of med school, and his uncle was a friend of Martha's. The uncle had told Martha that he had a nephew who needed an apartment. She invited them for drinks at the Jupiter before she would let him see it. He wasn't a drinker, but his uncle had told him to order a whiskey and drink it like a man or he wouldn't get the apartment. He did what he was told, but Martha saw that it was a difficult task and ordered him a light beer for the next round. She told him she could guess what anyone drank after just five minutes of conversation, and he was no whiskey drinker. He got the apartment anyway. No one really knew why.

Diane told us a story about breaking the news of her pregnancy to their aunt. Martha had cried and placed her hands on Diane's swollen belly as if to bless it. Wally wept a little. The others shared their stories, and the moment came for the ashes to be thrown over the edge.

"With the wind," Alice said to Wally. No one wanted ashes in their faces.

He moved to a better position on the boat and pulled out the Styrofoam plug, shaking the contents into the water. They floated on the surface in a stream of gray debris. He gave one final shake, and *splash!* The jar went into the water. It floated for a moment, upside down like the boat in *The Poseidon Adventure*, then bobbed sideways and sunk.

"Oh shit," Wally said calmly.

"Oh shit?" yelled Elliot. "That was a fifteen hundred dollar jar! You just threw fifteen hundred dollars into the ocean, you dumb shit!"

"Dude!" Jason yelled. "Settle down. It wasn't your jar."

"Shut your mouth, you stupid moron!" Elliot shouted.

Sam was trying to restrain Elliot now, hands on both of his shoulders.

"What is wrong with you?" Sam said into his face with worry. He pulled him to the opposite side of the boat and made him sit. Elliot was stiff with rage.

We were all surprised by the outburst. I looked at my sister and started laughing. Uncontrollably, snorting-crying-laughing. We knew it was bad timing, so Alice comforted me as if they were tears of sadness. No one bought it.

The group had planned to lunch at a restaurant in the town of Tiburon, a tiny peninsula that juts out into the bay on the north side in Marin County. It was popular with the sailing crowd and always busy. Alice had reserved a large outdoor table overlooking the docks. The silence was awkward until the cocktails arrived.

I watched tan sailors pull in and unload for beer and burgers and wondered what the cold people were doing now. My poor kids were stuck in the house for weeks at a time because it hurt their skin to go outside.

Elliot was moping like a spoiled child.

"I know he's supposed to be having a hard time with Martha's death, and his head injury and all, but come on...it didn't belong to him," I said to Jason quietly.

"That was the jar Martha bought from him the first time they met," Sam explained to me apologetically.

I know already! I wanted to say back. Sympathy had never been my strong point.

After a beer or two, some of Elliot's bitch wore off. Before you knew it, the table was loose and talkative, and I was almost having fun.

I found it interesting that Myles and Sophie were there. I wondered if anyone had told them they were evicted.

They were fairly quiet during lunch. Sophie was working Dan more aggressively than usual. Myles drank heavily, seeming distracted and aloof. Dan was pulling a sort of boyfriend thing on Sophie. He was sitting close, his body language was way too intimate, and he was smug about it. It was very strange to me that Myles was allowing it to happen, but I couldn't tell where he was in his own head.

Diane told us they would not be moving into the apartment. They were buying a house soon, she said, in Mill Valley.

"She is so full of shit," Alice whispered. "They can't buy a new car, let alone a house in Mill Valley."

"I didn't even know they were back together," I whispered back. "Maybe she doesn't want to live in the apartment where her aunt was murdered." I thought about the body lying there on the fireplace hearth, and my mouth twisted involuntarily.

After lunch, we boarded the boat and sailed across the bay. The wind had subsided, and I leaned back and enjoyed the warm sun on my face. The water was crowded with a weekend regatta of boaters. The iconic span of towering steel seemed to protect us from the rugged water outside the bay. We steered back toward the grand little city with its hills covered in white.

"No wonder it costs so much to live here. It's worth every penny," I said.

"If you see the dragon jar bobbing around, let me know and I'll jump in," Elliot joked, interrupting my peaceful moment. Funny what a little time and a lot of booze will do for the mood. Myles was bombed and grabbed the life preserver.

"Ready, Elliot?" He pretended to throw it overboard.

"Put that down, Myles." Sophie was in no mood for his antics.

"Yes, Your Highness." He bowed.

Alice and I locked eyes and smiled. I wondered if they had heard us calling her Princess or if it was just her natural title.

When we pulled into the marina, I told Alice and Jason I felt like walking.

"I'd go with, but these shoes are killing me," Alice said.

As I crossed the enormous lawn of the marina and headed up the hill over Fort Mason, I was touched with the guilt of my lies. I reminded myself that I was an adult and could do what I wanted. I thought of the words I'd always told my kids: if you're ashamed of it, it's not worth doing. I hadn't actually done anything wrong by meeting with Erik—nothing to be ashamed of anyway, so why the secrecy? I knew I was lying to myself, even at that moment.

The red-tile roofs of the abandoned military barracks now covered artists' workshops and rental spaces for start-up companies. I took the cypress-lined path to the top of the hill where the bay stretched out before me like a favorite friend. I could see the old neighborhood as

I came down the trail, even spotting the roof and back stairs of our old house. I ended in Aquatic Park shortly before three and sat on the concrete terraces that faced the water making an outdoor theater. A drum circle had formed, and I listened while I waited for the detective.

"How was your voyage?" he asked, arriving at exactly three.

He was wearing a light blue polo shirt, gray chinos, and a black Columbia zip-up fleece. I wondered if a woman had told him to stick to those colors.

"Hilarious and disturbing," I said, filling him in on the details of the day.

"Why do you think he was so mad about the stupid jar?"

"I don't know. Maybe it's all getting to him. It's been a tough week. He loses his close friend, then the fall..."

"Getting back to our last conversation...what did you mean with the Ted Bundy comment?"

"Elliot told me about the PermaNet," I said.

"Did he call it a Ted Bundy thing, or did you?"

"He did. And I did." I didn't know what he was getting at. "Is that what you had to talk to me about?"

"Just do me a favor and don't mention that again, okay? It's critical that those details stay private in order for us to catch this person," he said.

I nodded my head. "Okay, not a word. Elliot was pretty worried about me spilling it too. I haven't told anyone. Why the cop at the house?"

"There's a murderer on the loose."

"Jeez. We were attacked when we were away, and now we're back in the murder complex."

I filled him in on what had happened at Memorial Park. "I know it sounds paranoid, but I saw the guy watching us earlier that day. I think he was stalking us."

"Did you recognize him?"

"No, he looked like a serial killer. Dark clothes. Baseball cap hiding his face."

"Is that the uniform of a serial killer?" He grinned.

"Yes, you should know that in your line of work," I said, smiling. "Seriously, this guy was stalking us in the woods—at night! If it weren't for my incredible pipes and crazy sisters, who knows what he would have done. He left the park right after the attack—in a hurry, according to the ranger. Something was up for sure. I thought it might be Myles, but he got there before us, so he had to just be some creep, right?"

"Who knew you were going camping?"

"There are no secrets in the compound. They all could have known." After a moment of silent thought, I said, "I've had this theory about someone, but I don't think he could be the murderer. He's not the murdering type."

"Everyone is the murdering type."

"Here we go again. I don't believe that. Not everyone is cut out for it."

"People lose it sometimes. We're all capable. I've seen kind old ladies do it. I've seen children do it. We are all capable."

I thought about what buttons would have to be pushed for me to snap like that. It was easy: hurt my kids or family, I'd kill you, no problem.

"So what's this theory?" he asked after letting my mind go there for a moment.

"Could you kill?"

"I have killed, Lee," he said dismally.

We were quiet for a moment while we both considered this. I wondered what it was like to kill a person and if he was sorry. I wanted to ask him who it was and if there was more than one, but I didn't.

"So tell me about your theory," he said.

"I think Sam Larkin is Harry Byrne's son."

"Continue."

"Martha broke up Harry's first marriage. Well, that isn't exactly fair, is it? Martha and Harry broke up Harry's first marriage, to a woman named Jane. Jane left San Francisco after the split, probably pregnant, and moved to Oregon. Sam is just the right age and grew up in Portland."

"Have you talked to Sam about this?"

"No. But I wonder if Martha knew," I thought out loud.

"It's a pretty deep secret to keep but doesn't exactly provide a motive."

"Yeah, why now? If he wanted her dead, he's had years. I wonder if he looks like Harry. If he does, she had to have known. Plus, she left the building to the foundation. His foundation."

"Maybe he wanted the money for himself."

"I don't think Sam operates that way. Elliot, definitely, but not Sam."

We were quiet for a moment, looking out at the bay. I closed my eyes and let the sun touch my face. I could feel him watching me and felt a little heat from the attention. I wished he would lean over and kiss me. I knew it was bad, but with the alcohol and the sun and him next to me…that was what I wished, just for a moment. A stolen kiss like in my teenage years.

"I grew up on that hill behind us, you know," I told him, eyes still closed, and leaning back.

"Nice neighborhood."

I thought I sensed a little sarcasm in his voice. It was a nice neighborhood, even nicer now. I'd looked up how much apartments were, thinking we could keep one there, and the rent was six thousand dollars a month for a one bedroom.

"Are you from the city?" I asked him.

"Yeah. The Sunset with all of the other Irish Catholics."

The Sunset was a neighborhood on the northwest side of town. It lined the western end of Golden Gate Park and was truly the foggiest neighborhood in San Francisco. If you lived there, you'd better like your world gray. It was close to the beach, though, and had some great little streets lined with old-timey bars and restaurants.

"It's changed so much," I said. "I went to look for my favorite pizza place down there, and it was gone. I couldn't read a single sign. They were all in Chinese."

"Yes, it's the next generation's turn."

I liked his open mind. I knew people who had grown up in the Sunset who were infuriated by the takeover. San Francisco had always had one of the best Chinatowns in the country, but the Asian population now exceeded thirty percent, and some felt that was too much. I had a bigger problem with the SUV-driving yuppies who parked on the sidewalks, drove the property values sky-high, and honked like they were from New York, which they probably were.

I didn't feel like telling him about my parents, about how they died and how I called 911 before crawling in bed with my mother and crying next to her until they came to take her away. I wasn't in the mood to tell him about the day I figured out that there was no God. Or the year I started paying special attention to the news. People lost their entire families. Women lost all of their children. There was nothing fair about life. If God was that cruel, I wanted nothing to do with him.

"What do you believe, Erik?" I asked him.

"I believe in God. I see him all the time."

"Really?" I pulled my sunglasses down to look at him.

"Not literally, but in people who do good things for others."

"People suck," I said.

"Wow. A bit jaded there?"

I laughed. "I've been living on the East Coast for the past eight years. Trust me, they suck. You can't even change a lane without them honking and flipping you off. I've almost been killed over a lane change out there." I didn't realize my dislike wasn't true until I said it out loud. I knew so many wonderful East Coasters.

"What about your sister and the work she does? Or Sam?" He knew them all pretty well at this point.

"My sisters are angels. So is Sam." I started thinking about my life again. "There is no God, Erik. Trust me on that. If there were, he'd fix the mess he made. Do you know that every thirty seconds a child dies from malaria, a disease that only poor people get? Every thirty seconds a poor child dies from waterborne illnesses from not having access to clean drinking water. Did you know that?"

"No. I didn't know that. How is that God's fault?"

"How is it not?"

"There is enough of everything to go around this planet. Man is the one who doesn't distribute it well," he said.

"You sound like a socialist, Mr. Healy."

"No, just a Catholic. It's been tough to watch the rich getting richer and the poor getting poorer around here. The city's changed. I think the country's changed."

My phone rang. It was Alice. I ignored the call but let Erik know I had to be on my way. We walked together until it was awkward; at each new corner, we stopped like it was our last, finding one more thing to talk about until I finally tore myself away and went on alone. Giddiness and guilt made a toxic cocktail that I couldn't seem to put down.

CHAPTER 17

SAM AND ELLIOT HAD AN outdoor living room in front of their sliding doors. On a large jute carpet sat a love seat, two large chairs, and a coffee table. A cluster of Asian lanterns hung from the beam that supported the upstairs balcony, creating a chandelier over the table. Black and white pillows and a red wool throw were tossed to the side of a chair where Sam sat sipping scotch while reading a legal journal.

He looked small and delicate in the overstuffed chair. He was wearing a vintage wool cardigan, the kind with the thick folded collar that led to the brown leather buttons, giving him a professorial demeanor. His gray hair was thin and cut short. The soft wrinkles around his eyes and mouth conveyed his gentle spirit.

"Hey, Sam. How is Elliot feeling?" I asked when I saw him outside.

"He's better, thanks. Not sleeping much though. I gave him an Ambien and he's out. This has been really tough on him."

"Can I sit for a moment?"

"Sure. Can I get you something? Scotch?" he pointed to his own glass.

"Uh…I don't want to bother you." I might have preferred bourbon, but I'd never said no to a scotch.

"It's no bother. Sit." He went into the apartment, returning with a bottle and an elegantly etched rocks glass that matched his own. He was like a guest in his own home, sleeping on the expensive sheets and drinking from the elegant glasses but incognizant of their value.

"Well, you have some stories to tell when you get home," he said. We both smiled.

"Sam, I have to ask you something."

"Ask away," he said sincerely but with a look of curiosity.

"Are you Harry Byrne's son?" I was nervous that he was going to be angry with me for asking, but he wasn't. He smiled and leaned back in his chair.

"Yes, I am, Lee, but how the hell did you know?"

"This old boyfriend of Martha's at the funeral told me that Martha dumped him for Harry. He mentioned that Jane left suddenly and that she was pregnant. I wondered what had happened to the child. Then Wally told me that Jane lived in Portland, which is where you said you grew up."

"Mom died twelve years ago."

"I heard. I'm sorry. It sucks to be an orphan," I said.

"You know all about that, don't you?"

"Did Martha know who you were?" I asked.

"My guess is that she did, but we never talked about it. I look like him, or so they say. Elliot talked a lot about Martha when they first met. He'd arranged for me to meet her over cocktails. She spent a lot of time looking at me and asked me a couple of questions about where I grew up, my parents, the usual things you would ask someone you had just met. But she also asked me if I was happy, if I'd liked my father...questions that were a little weird for a first-time meeting.

"I didn't know anything about my birth father, except that he was dead. That's what they had told me. But I suspected there was more to the story because no one would ever tell me anything about him. My mother finally told me the truth on her deathbed."

"Wow. That must have been really confusing for you."

"Yes, confusing is the right word. First I thought I wanted to find him. But I had a great father growing up, and it felt like a betrayal. My dad passed away before my mom. He was a wonderful man. There was never a day when he didn't treat me like I was his child. It couldn't have been easy to accept a gay kid, especially back then. I was so lucky. So many kids have to hide their true selves. I told you about Elliot's mother, right? She's still waiting for him to find a nice girl so he doesn't go to hell."

We both laughed.

"So how did you figure it out?"

"Someone mailed me a photo of Harry and my mom. On the back it said, 'Harry and Jane Byrne, 1954.' I look a lot like him. I knew why she couldn't keep her eyes off of me that first night."

"Did you ask her if she sent it to you?"

"No, I never did, and I never will now, will I? I figured if she wanted to have a conversation about it, she would have. But it's a hell of a small world."

"Do you think that's why she left this place to your organization?" I asked.

"Maybe. She was always close to the issue. It was such an incredible act of kindness. I am still really floored that she did it." He was so sincere in his statement.

"You're a really good human, Sam. I don't get to meet many, but you restore my faith in humanity," I told him.

"Thanks, Lee." He was a little uncomfortable with the compliment. "I try. I would really appreciate it if you didn't talk to anyone about this. Elliot doesn't know, and he's going to be really pissed that I've kept it from him."

"Detective Healy knows," I confessed. "I'm sorry, Sam."

"Okay then." He thought for a moment. "It's time for it to come out apparently." He shrugged.

"Wally's your cousin." I grinned.

"It's occurred to me many times." He smiled.

So all the time that Sam lived there, he lived under his father's roof. And with the woman who destroyed his family. Talk about a motive for murder. But divorce happened all the time, and it didn't usually end with kids killing their stepparents.

Or does it? I asked nobody really but was thinking of Erik Healy. There he was again.

I wondered if the detective would see Sam the way I did. It definitely didn't look good for him. It was so obvious to me that Sam wouldn't hurt a fly. Erik's earlier words rang in my head. *Everyone is capable of murder.* I wondered what Elliot was going to say when he found out Sam had been keeping this secret from him.

Alice was taking a nap when I returned to the apartment. I grabbed my book and headed down to the Jupiter. Jason was working behind the bar. Wally, Diane, and the baby had stopped in. It was quiet inside, and Tabitha was running laps up and down the place. Diane planted herself next to me. *So much for reading*, I thought. Jason brought me a bourbon and soda without my having to ask.

"Hi, Lee. How is Alice doing?" Diane asked.

She was dressed in her usual cloak of invisibility: T-shirt with a stain on the front and a pair of capris that had never seen an iron. The T-shirt was a faded baby blue and matched her washed-out eyes. Her naturally blonde hair was as tired as the rest of her. I wondered if she could still be pretty, or if she ever was. The bones were there.

"Hi, Diane. Good to see you. Alice is exhausted and pretty sad."

"I didn't know she and Martha were so close."

Did I sense jealousy?

"How are you guys doing with all of this?" I asked her.

"Wally has been pretty upset, but Tabitha is the one who is really taking it hard. She's not sleeping; her appetite is down. It's so sad for her. She keeps asking for Ma-ta. That's what she called her."

"So they spent a lot of time together?"

"Oh yes. Ma-ta loved her Tabitha."

Somehow I just couldn't picture it. Martha reminded me of the kind of woman who would have declined the party invitation but would never have forgotten to mail a gift. I remembered that Diane was full of shit.

"And what about you? This must have been pretty tough on you with Wally being questioned and all."

"It was horrible. It was almost the end of us. But maybe it was for the best. He hasn't been drinking since. Do you think people can stop cold turkey like that without help? I wish he would get help."

"I don't really know, Diane," I said, then sipped my drink. She ran after the baby, who was now heading toward the back door.

I opened my book and plunged in before anyone could interrupt. Some books are good but can be great if read at just the right time. *A Moveable Feast* was filled with tales of hunger and poverty and love. Hemingway was fearlessly young and optimistic, writing about his first wife with the fondness of a widower, although in truth he had broken her heart. I believed that he spent his entire life regretting it. *Was it betrayal that had poisoned him in the end?* I wondered.

Diane sat next to me again before I could think about my own question.

What did she want? Maybe she's a phantom, I thought, looking at her.

I wondered if she had a soul, if there was anything beyond the dull blue eyes. A friend had told me about his "Phantom Theory": If you're driving down the road past cars full of people, those people and cars won't exist once out of your sight. They are gone. Soulless beings. They serve no purpose. Placeholders. I wondered this of a lot of people. Sometimes neighbors, sometimes crowds, sometimes people I met who seemed to be vacant.

Are you a phantom? Will you disappear once out of my line of sight? Would anybody miss you? Do you think about anything outside of yourself?

I could be one too, I realized when I thought about how judgmental I was. *Maybe I am the one saying nothing, and she is the one who is really living.* I thought of my kids, far away. *They don't really need me much anymore. Who am I? Do I save people? Create? Inspire? I am here just like Diane. We are the same.*

The baby was crying. She had tripped on a barstool during one of her laps. Before we could speak, her mother ran to her and held her tight. "Daddy, look, she misses Ma-ta," she said to Wally.

"Fuck me," I mumbled.

Two drinks, two more chapters of *A Moveable Feast.* Happiness. Freedom. Hemingway did whatever he wanted, when he wanted. I envied the ability to roam borderless through a city and not have to answer to anyone. I was always answering to someone.

Walking through the alley, I realized that at that moment, I didn't answer to anybody. No one was looking for me. The rarity of the freedom felt wasted on a return to the compound. I paused at the door and then kept walking. I headed past new construction with pits and cranes and dirt dug up from another San Francisco, passed a homeless guy pushing his belongings to nowhere, then stepped over a man who pissed himself while he slept on the sidewalk. I headed toward the bay, passed by four Starbucks coffee shops, two trendy restaurants, and a lady wearing a plastic garbage bag who claimed someone stole her clothes.

I reached Red's Java House and, instead of ducking in, went around to the back of the waterfront saloon and squeezed into the hole in the fence that was meant to keep people off the old crumbling pier. I lay on my back and closed my eyes while I listened to the rhythm of the cars as they hit the gaps in the decking above me until it lulled me to sleep.

When I woke up, it was dark. My phone was ringing.

"Hello?"

"Jesus Christ, Lee! Where the hell are you!" Alice yelled.

"Sorry. I fell asleep."

"What! Where are you? Jason said you left the bar hours ago."

"I went for a walk and I fell asleep."

"That makes a lot of sense, Lee. Really. Lacy is on her way. Did you forget about dinner?"

I squeezed back through the fence, leaving my crumbled concrete sanctuary behind and headed back to the murder place.

"Dummy!" Alice said when I came in.

"Dumber," I mumbled.

I got ready fast so I wouldn't be late and have to listen to Lacy tell me how I needed rehab.

I was leaving in a few days. It didn't seem possible for a trip to fly by so fast. At the same time, I was missing my family, my bed, even my pain-in-the-ass dogs.

Lacy called from the alley, and we headed out. Sophie came out of her apartment, and we met at the top of the stairs. I would have thought we were covered in vomit by the look on her face.

"Hi, Sophie," I said.

"Oh please," she said and cut a path down the stairs before us. She was wearing a short green polo dress and green flip-flops, and her hair was in a tight bun.

"Oh please what, Sophie?" my sister asked.

Sophie kept walking.

"Oh please what, Sophie?" Alice demanded.

She got to the door of the cottage and then said, without looking at us, "You got what you wanted, I'm out. I don't have to be nice to you anymore. I never liked you anyway."

The door opened before she knocked, and Dr. Shame Love looked out to see whom she was talking to.

Alice laughed. "Sophie, you have not been kind to me for one single second since you met me. Not one!" She yelled the last sentence like a crazy woman.

I just stood there, tired and very shocked. Everyone has a breaking point. Apparently Alice was cracking a little.

She was still enraged when we got in the car.

"Do you like how she waits until she is right in front of the door before she answered me? I don't have to be nice to you anymore? She made me feel like an unwanted houseguest from the moment she met me!"

"You're so scrappy. Settle down. What do you think she wants from him?" I asked.

"I have no idea. It's so pathetic how he is with her—how all men are with her. I don't get it!"

"She's probably blowing him right now," I said. I got petty when I was with my sisters.

"Why would she? There's nothing in it for her," Alice reminded me.

I thought about that and couldn't think of a reason she'd need Dan. "Maybe she just likes the attention, y'all," I said in my terrible Southern accent.

"Ah think I'll tawlk like this for the rest of the night, y'all. Maybe the men'll like me bettah," Alice said.

And so we did. Lacy was ready to slap us both but eventually found herself doing it too. We left the waiter a big tip for tolerating it.

"Nine a.m., girls, got it?" Lacy reminded us later, when she dropped us at the door to Alder.

"That doesn't mean eight forty-five, sister," I answered back.

She drove off, and we entered the courtyard as Sophie was running up the stairs.

"So busted!" I whispered, knowing I was being an ass.

"You're back a little late, Princess." Alice could not help herself.

"Mind your own business," she said.

Her hair was falling out of its neat bun, and I couldn't see her face to tell you if she had black smudgy whore eyes or not.

"Are you kidding me?" Alice said loudly before we even got to the door. "Can that man be that stupid?"

"I figured she was just borrowing something. Wow." I could not figure out what I had just seen.

"Where the hell is Myles? He's not out to sea for another week," Alice was thinking out loud. "She usually waits until he's gone to screw around on him."

"Hey, let's go to the Jupe for a nightcap," I suggested.

The thing I loved about Alice was that she was always up for anything. We headed back down the stairs. The cottage lights were dim.

"Could she really have?" I asked Alice.

"Not unless she wanted something. What could she want?"

"Yuck. How could you fuck clog man? Unless he has something on her…"

"He's a nice guy, Lee," Alice said, laughing. But the idea of the two of them grossed her out too. I knew it.

"Really, Alice? Everyone is so nice. One of those nice people took out Martha, remember?"

The bar was winding down from a busy Saturday night. We were able to get two stools next to each other. Alice and I both leaned over and kissed Jason hello, then I ordered a bourbon. My nap on the pier had given me an extra boost, and I was full of unspent energy. I felt eyes on me and was surprised to see Erik Healy looking down from a few seats away.

I smiled and waved. "Damn, he's cute," I whispered. I thought he might have read my lips.

He came over and stood next to my sister. "Hello, Harding girls."

"That's Harding women, Detective," Alice said.

He looked me toe to head and said, "Women, definitely."

What the...? I thought. It was either my drink or his or both, but I got that tingly feeling to the tips of my fingers again.

"Are you trolling for murderers this evening?" Alice was being kind of a bitch.

"Apparently they hang out here." He smiled. I almost spit my drink out. Alice didn't find it funny.

I gave her my "what's up?" look.

She nodded "nothing" back, but snottily, letting me know she wasn't happy about him.

I had a few drinks in me and gave her my "whatevah!" look back.

Erik watched us with a grin that showed he could speak our language.

"Want to meet for coffee again tomorrow?" he asked me, continuing to look straight into my eyes. Super intense.

"Are you drunk? What do you mean 'again?'" Alice asked.

"She's been helping me with the case."

He was drunk. He'd lost all of the uptightness that he carried so stoically. I liked it.

"Excuse me." Alice stood up, gave me a squinty-eyed dirty look, and headed down to the end of the bar, where she chatted with someone she recognized.

I looked at Erik and said, "Had a few tonight, Tattletale?"

He didn't take her seat but instead moved closer to me, standing in between my legs. I was looking up at him, and he still wasn't taking his eyes off me. I did look really cute in my favorite black sleeveless wrap shirt and a pair of black slacks with the cutest silver sandals ever made.

He looked me over again.

"We went out for dinner tonight," I said like I needed to explain.

"You look very nice," he said, not taking his eyes off me.

"Thanks. Do you come here often?" I honestly couldn't think of anything else to say. I looked up at him, feeling like a teenager. We both started laughing, but he didn't let go of the eye lock.

"I had a blind date earlier. It was unbearable," he said. "I needed a drink afterwards, and I only live a few blocks away. I used to come here often before the dot-com thing. It's always crowded now."

"Blind dates. Another great thing about being married."

I loved being married, and I was happy, I told myself again.

"So you're happy?"

"Blissfully." It was kind of a last-ditch effort to repel him—a weak one. I felt bad for saying it, remembering so clearly what it was like not to have a partner in life. He still wasn't standing back, and I still wasn't asking him to. But his intensity faded, and I missed it immediately. I wondered—not for the first time—if I owed my husband one for his transgression so many years ago and decided I didn't.

"I think I'll have another bourbon." I looked to the bar, but before I could, he signaled Jason, who poured me another.

"Myles was in here earlier. He was on a mission. I had to cut him off," Jason told us without a single judgmental eye toward our proximity to each other.

"That doesn't make any sense at all," I said. "We saw Sophie slink into Dr. Dan's place tonight, and she didn't look like she was borrowing an egg."

"Those two are sick," Jason said and made his way down to the other end of the bar. I wondered if he couldn't bear to watch. He and Jack got along great.

"He's not kidding," I said. "We caught her coming out tonight. She was not as well put together as she was when she went in."

"Maybe they were watching a movie and she fell asleep?" he suggested. No one could really believe Sophie would get together with Dan.

"Maybe," I said, then I added, "while her abusive boyfriend ties one on here? It doesn't make any sense."

All this murder talk had killed the mood and we lost that magic moment. I could still feel the heat though. Alcohol and Erik Healy didn't mix. He was wearing a silver-gray, perfectly pressed shirt and flat-front black slacks.

"You're very cute, Detective." I looked him straight on to tell him, and he didn't skip a beat.

"So are you, Mrs. Harding. I wish you didn't have a husband."

"Maybe I wouldn't be so attractive if I didn't. What was wrong with the girl tonight?"

"She wasn't you."

Oh shit, I thought. *You are playing with fire.*

"What I'd like to do is take you home so you could have coffee at my place tomorrow." He smiled. "You wouldn't even have to get out of bed."

"Hmmm," was all I could say, while I shook my head with a weak, "No."

He moved closer, and just when I panicked at the thought that he might try to kiss me, he put his face next to mine and inhaled deeply.

"You smell so nice," he whispered. "I just want to breathe you in."

I could smell him too. Not too clean, and so manly.

"You're killing me," I whispered back.

Alice caught us mid-sniff, and pretty much yanked me out of my chair and back to the apartment.

CHAPTER 18

I THOUGHT DRUNKEN FANTASIES ABOUT Detective Healy until I passed out cold. I had a massive headache when I woke up, and the reality of what I'd done the night before hurt even more than my head. I called my husband first thing to tell him how much I loved him.

"Did you have fun with your sisters last night?"

"Too much. How are the boys?"

"Good. Still sleeping. Surprised?"

"Not at all. Tell them I love them and to call me when they wake up."

"What are you doing today?"

"Lacy is taking us to the wine country."

"I am so jealous," he said for the millionth time since I had arrived.

"I'm sorry you couldn't be here for the murder. You would have really enjoyed that too," I joked.

"Yeah, nothing really exciting ever happens around here. Oh! I stepped in dog shit yesterday. That was exciting."

Overwhelmed with guilt, my head dropped back onto the pillow in a pain that I felt was deserved. I loved that man to death. We had a good life together, but marriage was fragile. Life was fragile. I knew that better than most. I said good-bye to Jack with an extra dash of guilt-induced tenderness.

I heard Lacy coming up the stairs and ran to the bathroom. She was ten minutes early and looked like a million bucks in a sleeveless, V-neck cashmere sweater and pressed jeans.

"Did you actually iron your jeans, sister?" I asked her.

"Did you actually comb your hair?" she replied back and kissed me.

Alice came out last with a backpack full of drinks and snacks.

"I can't stop thinking of the Princess and the Clog," I said in the car.

"That is hilarious." Alice gave me a courtesy laugh, then added, "I can't stop thinking about you whoring it up with that uptight detective."

"What?" Lacy asked.

I filled her in on Sophie and Dan's night together, hoping Alice would leave it alone, but she didn't.

"After seeing Sophie sexed up last night, we needed a drink. So we went to the Jupe. Detective Tighty Whities was there and started humping Lee. Then they made out in the bar."

"Shut up, Alice!" I said, laughing. "You fucking tattletale!" I added. "He did not hump me. But he did smell me, and I let him. Oh, and he asked me to go home with him."

"He did not!" Alice yelled.

"Want to know what's really scary? All I could think about was how clean his sheets would be. No dog hair on those babies."

I didn't tell them that my blood boiled over and I almost said yes, or that I was still thinking about what it would be like, or that I would have gone had Alice not saved me.

"I can't remember the last time someone asked me to go home with them," said Lacy.

"I can't remember the last time you got too drunk at a bar," I said.

"I can. I married him," Alice reminded us, and we all laughed.

"This is why I need to come home. Right now!" I said. I never laughed like that in New Jersey. I complained and swore and felt crushed by the weight of the weather and congestion and speed of life. I winced at the harsh accents and long fingernails. I wanted to slap people when I heard them say "Youz guys" to their children. I spent the winter wishing for spring, then spring came, and it rained for two months until one day it was muggy and ninety degrees. Fall finally arrived, and I pushed winter back, knowing I would sink into misery again, and poof! My life was going past me with nothing but complaining and wishing and people who had learned to survive it by pushing, pushing, pushing through.

I had come to learn that women were important to me, maybe because I was so close to my sisters. They knew everything and still loved me. I felt sorry for women who didn't have sisters. You learned the best things about friendship from them: forgiveness, loyalty, honesty, and truth. Nothing got by my sisters.

Lacy wove the car onto the Golden Gate Bridge. The double peaks were missing in the fog. The water was clear and speckled with sailors enjoying the last day of the weekend. Through the arches of the bridge, the green headlands of Marin pulled us forward with their calm curves and soft hills.

"Maybe Dan knows something?" I said, still thinking about the weird encounter with Sophie.

"I was thinking that too. Maybe it was a bribe fuck?" Alice replied.

"You guys are assuming they had sex. What if they hung out and watched a movie?" Lacy said.

"That's what Erik said."

"Oh, 'Erik' again."

"Shut up, Alice," I said, more snottily than usual because she was right.

"Well, it makes sense, doesn't it? Maybe she and Myles got in a fight. He went to the bar and drank away his sorrows. She went to Dan's for a shoulder to cry on," Lacy suggested, ignoring the antics.

"I don't know. She really looked like she was up to something and was definitely trying not to get caught on her way back up the stairs. Don't you think, Alice?"

"Definitely. She was mortified when we saw her on the way back. Why would she act like that if she were just at a friend's watching a movie?"

Pure warm sun wrapped around my face and neck, and I embraced it back, taking my sweater off so it could touch my shoulders. I was feeling alive and sensual, almost purring from the synergy of the last evening. Lacy turned the radio up, and I forgot for a moment about Sophie and Martha and my own family. I could only think of Erik. My entire mind and body were dedicated to imagining what could have been.

We pulled off the highway in Sausalito to take the top off and get some breakfast. The little town started at the water's edge, then carved its way up the steep hillside with some of the best views and most expensive real estate in the world. We took our bagels and coffee with us and walked down to the waterfront park to eat.

Lacy pulled out a wine-country map and charted out our day. We'd start at Chimney Rock in Napa and then work our way back to the square in Sonoma in time for a late lunch. Each winery was circled, and she had notes and printed reviews on their products.

"Remember when Mom and Dad used to bring us to Agua Caliente to swim?" Alice asked.

"I don't remember," I said sadly.

"You were little," Lacy said. "I'm not sure she was even born yet," she said to Alice.

I hated that they had so much more time with my parents than I had.

"Tell me about it. What was it like?" I asked.

Lacy was so patient with me, knowing that I wanted every detail of our former life. They were fading shadows to me. She told me about the size of the pools and which ice cream the snack bar had served and how my father loved to hold me in the water.

We sat on the grass, eating our breakfast in the sunshine and talking about our childhood.

"It was good that Martha didn't have children," I said out loud. "It must have been so much easier to die."

When we went to got back on the road, there was an accident on Highway 101 North, which caused all cars to stop. After an hour of baking in the sun, we turned the car around and headed back to the city.

"What should we do instead?" Lacy asked.

"Let's drop the car off and take a cab to North Beach?" Alice suggested.

When we got back to the alley, there were cop cars again.

"Shit."

"We live here," Alice told the police when they tried to stop us from getting in. "What's going on? Is everyone okay?" she asked nervously.

"We're just taking someone in for questioning. Everyone is fine," the young officer told us.

Lacy parked the car around the corner, and we got back in time to see Elliot being pushed into the backseat of a squad car. Sam stood there silently watching, in shock. Alice ran to his side and hugged him.

"Impossible. What is this?" she asked him.

"They're questioning him for Martha's death," Sam told us.

Sophie and Dan were standing together.

Where is Myles? I wondered.

Erik was leaning over, talking to the officer in the driver's seat. He glanced my way but didn't approach.

I gave him my "what the fuck?" look, but he didn't seem to notice.

"We just have a few questions," Erik assured Sam, trying to calm his shaken nerves. "He'll call you when we finish up."

Alice walked Sam back to his apartment, and I followed, looking around curiously at the décor once we were inside. The kitchen, which opened into the living room area, had Chinese orange-red shelving above the counters instead of cabinetry. Polished concrete floors were blanketed in antique Persian rugs. An enormous black-and-white watercolor of a horse by Chiura Obata hung on the main brick wall. I thought of my suburban home with a little bit of shame. It was filled with Pottery Barn-like crap from catalogs.

"Can I get you a drink, Sam?" Alice asked.

"Please. There's a bottle of scotch on the bar and glasses on the shelf above it."

"Do you need to call a lawyer or something?" I asked.

"I did. She's on her way there now."

"So what happened?"

"They came to the door asking for Elliot. When he came out, they marched past me and asked him to come with them. Just like that. They wouldn't tell me a thing."

"Why would they think Elliot killed Martha? What's the motive?"

"I have no idea. He loved her like a mother."

I couldn't help remembering Elliot's face when I told him he had shared the murder details with me. It was almost violent. I didn't have a hard time believing he was capable, I just couldn't figure out why he would do it. We would know soon enough.

"Do you want us to stay with you until they call?" Alice asked Sam.

"No thanks, Alice. I'm okay. Thank you, Lee. Really. I'm okay."

We said our good-byes and were about to head out for lunch when Sophie opened the door to her apartment and looked over the balcony railing.

"Have you guys seen Myles around?"

I was surprised she would even address us after the last evening, but she was completely frazzled. She had no makeup on, her hair was pulled back tight, and it occurred to me for the first time that her eyes were too big and looked like one of those postcards from the 1970s.

"No," Alice answered. "Is everything okay?"

She disappeared back over the rail without answering.

We took a cab to North Beach and had lunch at the Gold Spike, a classic old restaurant with red-checkered tablecloths and the same menu they'd had since 1950. We were drinking red wine poured from a carafe, which was the only wine they served, trying to figure out why Elliot was taken in.

"Maybe it has something to do with the sale of the bar?" I suggested.

"What would be in it for Elliot?" Lacy asked.

"A finder's fee maybe? I don't know. It doesn't seem worth killing a good friend over."

"He's the one who found her," Alice reminded us. "Maybe he went inside and killed her, then pretended to be upset."

"There is no way he did that to her," I said.

They both looked at me.

"Do you know how Martha was killed?" Alice asked.

"Yes. And you don't want to know. Trust me. I wish I didn't know."

"Lee, I can outgross you, remember?"

"This is different, Alice. She was your friend. Plus, I was sworn to secrecy."

"Are you kidding me? You and that detective share secrets!" She was furious.

"No! Elliot told me. He got too drunk at Martha's wake and spilled it. No one is supposed to know. I promised."

"Everyone is going to know soon enough."

So I told them.

"I don't think Elliot would do that," Alice said quietly. "You were right. I wish I didn't know."

The rest of our lunch was quiet. I made them go to the Savoy Tivoli for a drink for old times. Once we did that, we couldn't miss stopping at the Vesuvio for another. City Lights bookstore was right next door, so we browsed for a while. I purchased Helen Weaver's memoir of her times with Jack Kerouac. I loved memoirs, especially those about writers. Gossipy tales full of private insight...what's not to love? We stopped at Tosca for a "coffee." I had to say coffee to get Lacy there, but she was feeling festive and ordered an Irish coffee along with us. An older gentleman poured the drinks in an assembly-line manner. His formal white coat reminded me of a laboratory. Red leather booths lined the dark corners of the bar. The retro setting was made perfect by the glowing jukebox, which carried only Rat Pack standards. I put some money in and played "That's Amore."

"Three drinks in one day, Lacy. Should we check you in?" Alice joked.

"I can drink you both under the table," she replied. "I'm just not an alcoholic like you, so I don't feel the need." She wasn't kidding, and we both knew it.

"I'm good with being an alcoholic," I said.

I knew that drove her nuts.

Sam was gone when we arrived back at the complex. I wondered if Sophie had found Myles. The cop at Martha's door was gone. No need for security when the murderer was caught? Erik Healy called me later, but I didn't answer. He called again, and I declined the call again.

"Are we not talking?" he texted me.

"Were we ever?"

"I couldn't tell you, Lee."

"I shouldn't tell you a lot of things."

"Meet me at the stands."

"No. I think I need to stay away from you."

"I'm leaving now. You'll recognize me by my drum."

"I'll look for the guy with the cop hair."

"Nice. Does that mean you're coming?"

I told Alice I was going for a walk. I brought my book.

"Don't fall asleep while you're walking, Dummy," she said.

Jason was home tonight. I felt good about giving them some alone time.

I passed several more homeless people on the way down to Aquatic Park. I actually stepped over two who were sleeping miserably on the sidewalk.

In my younger years, one could be followed down the street, harassed for a dollar. I didn't see that anymore. Several years ago there was an ordinance passed to keep them from aggressively panhandling. It was like sticking a Band-Aid on a gunshot wound.

Erik was waiting for me on the stands, but we moved down to the water and sat on the beach.

"What happened with Elliot?" I asked.

"I had to bring him in, Lee. Just so he knew that I was watching him. I was worried about you being there."

"What are you talking about?"

"Elliot supposedly saw the murder scene for a minute, then freaked out, right? But he knew details that only the murderer could have known. I found it highly suspicious that he would know that Ted Bundy had done the same exact thing to one of his victims. And how did he know what brand of hair spray Martha used? Who knows that?"

"I knew about the Ted Bundy thing."

"You did?"

"Yes, I'm obsessed about those kinds of gruesome details. Alice would know too. We're kind of intrigued by the macabre."

He looked at me, and I wondered if he just lost all attraction.

"And the hair spray? Come on? He'd probably borrowed it from her before." I knew Elliot would have his own salon-brand hair spray—he was not a PermaNet kind of guy—but I said it anyway. "What's his motive for killing Martha? She was a good friend of his."

"There's been a lot of deception. Elliot knew that Harry was Sam's father. He figured it out when he was snooping around Martha's place while she was out of town. He was supposed to be watering her plants. He saw a photo of Harry in her office, then dug further into her photo albums."

"The photo that was mailed to Sam!"

"Yes, he mailed the photo anonymously so that Sam would figure it out and claim his birthright, but Sam didn't mention the photo to Elliot, and Elliot couldn't say anything because only the person who mailed it could have known about it."

"So he never told Sam or Martha that he knew?"

"Elliot kept it very tight. The guy has a real sense of entitlement. It seems he felt like Martha owed them something. Meanwhile, he continued to go deeper and deeper into debt. His shop has been running on empty for some time now. His clients told him they would pay him a hefty finder's fee if he would convince Martha to sell the bar. Martha allowed him to look into it, but in the end, she wanted to keep it in the family."

"So you think that Elliot killed her for this?" I still could not believe it. "Did you look to see if he rented a Gocar?" I added quickly, wondering if that had been Elliot in the woods that night.

"What? No, Lee. I really don't believe those incidents are related."

"Well, I do. Why would Elliot want to hurt Alice or me? The person who did this had it out for one of us. Do you think he did it?" I asked him.

"We have no physical evidence in this case at all. The murder weapon was disposable. The assailant wore gloves. He's very neat. Elliot is emotional and messy. As soon as we started questioning him, he spilled his guts about everything. I can't see him pulling this off without leaving something behind."

"He's going to have a lot of explaining to do with Sam," I said, thinking of how hurt I would be if Jack had kept a secret like that from me.

"Yeah, the conversation between them started at the station. Sam's a very calm man, but he couldn't hide the look of betrayal."

"Great. Like it's not depressing enough at the compound. Can you imagine what it's going to be like now? Martha was found dead in her apartment, who the hell knows what kind of weird shit is going on between Sophie, Myles, and Dan, and now this? I'm glad I get to go home soon."

I saw a wince of disappointment when I said this.

"When do you leave?" he asked.

"I'm supposed to leave in a few days, but I'm not leaving my sister in that place until the murderer is caught."

"It must be very cold in New Jersey if you'd rather stay at Alder then go home."

"I don't really know where I belong anymore," I said, trying not to tear up.

He pulled me toward him, and I leaned in. He ran his hand through my hair, pulling it back from my face. We sat quietly, facing the water.

I knew it was hedonistic, but it felt so good to be touched by him.

A swimmer went past us while the fog rolled into the bay, covering it in dusk's cold blanket. The day's events, plus the three cocktails I had in North Beach, were weighing on me.

"I could fall asleep right now," I said. "But my sister told me not to while I am walking." I laughed the way you do at an inside joke.

I didn't want to move. It felt so good for the moment. My own hands never touched him back. Somehow I felt like that would cement the betrayal.

"Let's go up to the Buena Vista for a drink," I suggested, knowing our intimacy was going to get me into more trouble.

I pulled away, and we walked up the street to the old bar that claimed to have brought the Irish coffee to America. As a child, I'd sat with my dad while a guy with thick white hair and a silver handlebar mustache poured him the famous concoction, decades ago. I'd had my first here, poured by the same imposing figure, who'd remembered my dad and many of the other neighborhood fixtures he'd served over the years. Nothing had changed inside. The bar was filled with tourists, as usual. I supposed I was a tourist now.

"I've never been here," Erik confessed.

"This place serves so many drinks that there is a run on the coffee glasses they use," I told him. "They stash them in a warehouse somewhere, and none of the other bars can get their hands on the design."

My phone rang. It was my husband. I ignored it. It rang again. It was my sister. I ignored it again.

I was thinking about the trouble I was stepping into when Erik's phone rang. He looked to see who was calling, then apologized and stepped outside to take it.

He came back in with an obvious look of distress.

"I have to go."

"What is it?" I asked.

"Myles Alcazar is dead.

CHAPTER 19

ERIK PAID THE BILL AND we headed out. It was awkward. He had a car parked somewhere in the area, and I knew he had to go in a hurry. It was getting dark, and I thought he might feel like he had to give me a ride back.

I stuck my arm out and waved down the first cab that went by before I could give him a chance to object. I hopped in, and it drove off before we could have an awkward good-bye. I wondered what was happening on Alder. Was he found there? I called my sister.

"Where are you, Dummy? Jason is making dinner for us."

"I'm on my way now. Be there in five."

I brought my intense sense of dread with me into the courtyard. News had not hit Alder yet, and I certainly wasn't going to be the one to break it to them. When I arrived in the apartment, our meal was ready, and we sat down at the table almost immediately. There was fire in my stomach. I could hardly eat a bite of the macaroni and cheese Jason had prepared. I knew the ball was going to drop but couldn't find the guts to tell my sister that I had been with Erik this afternoon. She assumed my silence was caused by an early hangover from our long day of drinking.

"Myles is dead." I just spit it out. I couldn't stand it any longer. You couldn't tell me anything if you didn't want my sisters to know.

They both just looked at me.

"Myles is dead. They found him somewhere dead. That's all I know," I blurted out.

About two seconds later, there were footsteps on the stairs. Alice ran to the door to look. It was the police, heading to Sophie's apartment.

"Oh my God," my sister said. "Oh my God!" Then she looked at me. "Thanks for the notice, asswipe."

Sophie didn't take it well. She was moaning. It was the sound of the loss of a father, brother, companion, savior, lover. Sadness. Pain so pure that I felt it myself. I was sick from the noise. We all were. Sam was up the stairs immediately, looking tired and shocked like the rest of us.

"I so want to help her, but I'm not the right person to do it," Alice said.

This reminded me again about the importance of sisters. That's whom you called during these times. Alice and I stayed in the apartment. Jason ducked out to see if there was anything he could do.

I looked to the cottage. The lights were off except for the one lamp usually on when no one was home.

"Where did they find him? How?" Alice asked me.

"I have no idea. I didn't have time to ask. Erik just called and told me he was dead."

"He just called you and said, 'Hi, Lee. Myles is dead'?" Alice asked, looking at me incredulously.

"Something like that. I came back here immediately. I didn't know how to tell you."

"Was he murdered?"

"I don't know! I'm telling you I have no fucking idea," I was whisper-yelling so they wouldn't hear us on the balcony.

My thoughts turned to Sam and the horrible day he'd had. First he found out his partner had been betraying him, then his friend turned up dead. I filled my sister in on what I knew about Elliot and Sam.

"I just can't believe Elliot is capable of being so sneaky. Poor Sam must be heartbroken," Alice said.

"I wonder where Elliot is now."

"Probably at his crazy mother's house. That's a good start to his punishment."

"What's she like?" I asked.

"I've only met her once, but from the way Elliot and Sam describe her, she is really nasty."

"Is she bad enough to make him hate women with a vengeance?" I asked.

"I still can't see Elliot doing this. If she was hit over the head with the dragon jar or a size fourteen Jimmy Choo, I could see it, but I seriously doubt he would stick something in a coochee, you know?"

"But he made that comment about Ted Bundy. I mean, who else would know about that?"

"You!" She laughed.

"Or you," I reminded her. "I wonder if Elliot rented a Gocar."

"Why would Elliot attack you in Memorial Park, Lee? Think about it. He could do that here without traveling all that way."

"Maybe because he'd told me what he'd seen that night and knew it would implicate him."

She rolled her eyes like I was crazy.

I was quiet for a moment. I was thinking about how all those photos we had sent over the years were actually real people with real family and friends and lives.

"I wonder how Myles died," Alice said.

"We'll know soon enough."

Jason came home just before sunrise. He and Sam had gone with Sophie to the morgue to identify the body. Sam had given Sophie something to help her sleep and put her to bed. Then he and Jason went down to the courtyard to drink and talk until the light filled the sky.

I heard Jason come in and got up from the sofa bed. From the window, I saw Dan come into the courtyard wearing scrubs from his shift at the hospital. He walked like someone who had run a marathon, like it hurt to hold his own frame. I wondered if he would pretend to be upset about Myles. Alice was up now too, and we sat on her bed in our pajamas asking Jason about his night.

"He was at SF General. The morgue was just like you see in the movies. They had him on a table, covered with a sheet. They pulled the cover off for Sophie to identify him," he told us.

"How did he die?" I asked.

"Head trauma. One of the ship workers found him on a dock in Mission Bay. I'll bet he went to the Ramp after he left the Jupe, maybe got so drunk he fell and hit his head."

The Ramp was a waterfront bar in Mission Bay. It used to be crowded with young kids. It was never my scene. I didn't know what it was like now but pictured young dot-comers in their Patagonia vests.

"He liked to go there. He was trashed when he left he Jupiter. I can't imagine him drinking even more. He had a bruise on his face. Maybe he fought with someone at the bar? He gets pretty obnoxious when he drinks like that."

I found it ironic that a man who had beaten women could have possibly died from the ass kicking he deserved.

"Poor Sophie," Alice said.

"I know. I feel so bad for her…but what the hell was going on with them? Do you think they got in a fight, so she went to Dan for comfort? Is she that dependent on men?"

"Who knows? She's going to have to live with that though," Alice said.

CHAPTER 20

DAWN BECAME MORNING. ONE CUP of coffee wasn't enough. I was carrying the kind of exhaustion that only fell off with a nap. The courtyard was as quiet as the wet air that occupied it. Myles was gone. Elliot was gone. Martha was gone. I was supposed to leave soon. I couldn't think of leaving Alice without resolution. We thought about canceling breakfast with Lacy, but it wasn't like we could be any good to Sophie.

"I have to go over there and see her," Alice said.

"You're brave," I replied, thinking of their confrontational last meeting. It didn't seem to matter so much anymore.

Lacy came to get us for breakfast. She was appalled when we told her about Myles's death and told Alice it was time to move out.

"I'm not leaving my home," Alice sounded like a snotty teenager and realized it. "I'm sorry. I love living here, Lace. I'm not going to let some nut job chase us out."

"This place is hazardous to your health. Plus, what happens when Elliot comes back?"

"I don't see Sam letting him back in anytime soon. He took his key from him. He's really pissed off," Jason told us.

"He is now, but as soon as he misses him, he'll be back, and then you're in danger here again," Lacy proclaimed.

I kept thinking about the Gocar. It just didn't make any sense. Did Elliot attack us in the park? No one else seemed to think the incident was related to Martha's death, and I was beginning to think it might not be either.

"If Myles murdered Martha, and I don't think it's been ruled out, then the murderer is dead," I said.

I walked over to the fridge and pulled out a bag of caramels. "Want one?" I asked Lacy. I knew she would be annoyed, but I was feeling pretty confrontational about it. "I'm on fucking vacation, remember. I didn't sign up for a whodunit." I threw one to Alice.

"I didn't say anything," said Lacy, holding up her hands in defense.

"We're going to the Haight," I said. "When in Rome, Lacy. When in Rome."

I tossed her a caramel and could not believe it when she opened it up and took a little nibble.

"Oh for God's sake! Eat the damn thing. Don't waste it on a taste," Alice said.

We cabbed over to Haight Street for the best oatmeal and orange-rind French toast topped with pounds of fresh fruit and yogurt. The Haight was one of the few places in the city that was still a little funky. Not that it was untouched by gentrification. When I was a kid, we went there to trade our clothes at the secondhand stores, bought our rolling papers and bongs, and got our weed off the street from a dealer. On the way there, we had driven by a Gap store, and we could still buy weed, but legally, in a retail dispensary with custom wood décor and knowledgeable salespeople to help you. Most of the run-down Victorians had been restored by the new wealth, but the standards from the old days were still there. After breakfast, we headed down to Murio's Trophy Room and ordered Bloody Marys from the bartender, who was too busy doing his opening setup work to make conversation with us.

"I am so relaxed right now," Lacy said in a watching-the-stars kind of voice.

"I haven't been in here since Jesus went down the Nile in a basket," Alice was feeling nostalgic.

Lacy and I laughed.

"It was Moses, you dumb ass!" Lacy said.

It took her a minute.

"Oh yeah," Alice replied, laughing so hard at her own faux pas that tears were running down her face. "It was…" The bartender probably thought she was crying. "It was…" Her head was down on the bar, and she was snorting. "Moses," she finally spit out.

I could see how people became addicted to weed. It was the greatest enhancer. At it's best, forests glowed just a little greener and a tiny tickle could turn into the most uncontrollable laughter. I also knew I couldn't go on like this much longer. I valued my brain cells.

The bartender was watching us.

"We ate pot candy," Lacy confessed to him like she was proud of herself.

He ignored her because we were three old day drinkers and he was in the twilight of his youth.

"Cheers to being alive with my sisters!" I said, and we toasted to a day without death.

Golden Gate Park was always gray and cold. The city's early founders had speculated on the worst fog belt in the city, expecting it to take off like the Upper East and West Sides of Central Park in New York. They even hired Frederick Law Olmsted, one of Central Park's chief architects, to design the space. He had refused, saying there was no way he could work his magic on the arid sand dunes. That didn't discourage them, and they found William Hammond Hall willing to take on the challenge.

A century later, the sand had been tamed and a park began to take its unique shape. There was none of the moneyed magic of lush Central Park. Golden Gate Park was as tough as the spikes used to build the city. Drought and wind resistant, the land stretched from the roughest and coldest of beaches to the spot at the end of Haight where the sun started to win the war. Dig down a foot in any direction and I would find sand.

It was on the very spot that the Summer of Love took shape in 1967. Braless girls and drugged-out musicians met up with civil rights leaders and antiwar protesters to make San Francisco the hippie capital of the world. A cultural revolution took place there—it was sacred ground. Some of those soldiers were injured by drug abuse and mental illness. We passed by many of them on our way through the park. They asked for money or food, but mostly money.

San Franciscans did everything in the fog. I could remember playing in a neighbor's sprinkler in the gray mist. We didn't really get true seasons, but Mark Twain wasn't lying when he said that the coldest winter he had ever spent was a summer in San Francisco. That day we were walking two weather zones. I took the sweatshirt from around my waist and put it on, zipping it up all the way—wet wind was as bad as a snow flurry. When we hit the shelter of the trees, the gusts died down and the shivering stopped. Small paths led to open fields, lakes, and waterfalls.

A couple of times during the day, one of us would say, "Myles is dead." It was just so weird. We're here, then we're gone. Dead.

"Myles is dead. Dead on the docks. Deader than a doornail," Alice rambled.

"What the hell is a doornail?" I asked.

"Deader than Eddie Vedder," she continued.

"He's actually alive," I chimed in.

"Deader than I hope to get ever. Dead without meds. Dead like Jed," she was losing her mind.

"Dead in a bed. Dead giving head," Lacy added.

It went on like that for some time.

We made our way to the water and walked up the hill to the Cliff House, a historic old restaurant that overlooked the wild rocky waters outside the bridge, and caught a cab back to Alder. After the crazy and almost-sleepless night before, I was nap ready but dreaded the trip back to the death house. Alice was feeling the same way. Lacy offered to take us to her house, but Alice wanted to check on things at the apartment. My stuff was there, plus I had been hoping to meet up with Erik sometime that evening to get the story on Myles. He hadn't called all day. I hoped I would run into him.

The courtyard was blanketed with the stillness of tragedy, which was great for napping. I didn't even hear a toilet flush from Sophie's place. I thought about what it would be like to lose Jack. I didn't think I would be able to breathe. For better or for worse, Sophie had grown up in the arms of her protector, and now he was gone. She was so alone. No girlfriends or sisters to fall on. She had Elliot, but he had his own troubles at the moment. Sam was preoccupied. I doubted she would want to lean on Dan. He seemed to be such a big part of the story.

What was the story? I wondered.

I decided to go see her. I couldn't take the idea of anyone being so utterly alone. Alice was passed out, and Jason had left for the bar. I really had to push myself because I was afraid she would just slam the door in my face. I knocked softly and she answered, swollen-eyed, in a pair of sweats and a T-shirt.

"What do you want?" she said weakly and then just cried.

I gave her an awkward hug. She cried like it hurt, like every breath and every hiccup was painful.

"I'm so sorry for you, Sophie. I am so, so sorry. I can't even imagine your pain."

"Do you want to come in?" she asked.

She moved aside for me, and I stepped in. I hadn't seen her apartment before. It was as funky as the rest of them: wide-plank floors like next door, the same big industrial windows, concrete counter tops. It would have seemed cold except that there were brightly colored artifacts to warm it up. A mask collection from Africa, woven cloth from Central America, Day of the Dead figures, and colorful art were simply displayed. Sophie watched me look.

"Myles has been everywhere. These are the things he brought back to me. We talked about traveling together, but between school and my new job...I just really focused on getting ahead. I wanted to be independent." She chuckled sadly. "Be careful what you wish for."

Her books were sprawled out on the table. I wondered if she would be able to continue to study.

"I know you must think he was horrible, and I'm not making excuses for him. He had a terrible temper. But he was getting help. I told him, if he didn't, I would throw him out. He didn't know about Martha's ultimatum because I was going to tell her he was getting help. He didn't really hurt me that night that you heard us. I just made a huge deal out of it to teach him a lesson. I had no marks, and he really caught himself."

She paused for a moment. I thought she would cry again, but instead, she quietly spoke. "He was doing really well."

I couldn't really say anything that was going to help, so I just stayed silent for once. But then it was too quiet. Awkwardly quiet.

"Do you have family? Siblings?" I asked.

"I have a brother, but I haven't talked to him in years. I don't even know if he is alive. Myles was really all I had."

"What about your parents?"

"They were ridiculous excuses for adults. My father left when I was five and my brother, Mikey, was three. My mother was busy with men and alcohol. Total lush. I used to find her passed out on the sofa with a bottle in her hand. She crashed all of the family cars. Different men in the house all the time." She was speaking with a Southern accent, and I realized that remembering her childhood brought it back.

"I met Myles when I was fifteen. He rented a room in our house, and my mother tried everything she could to get him, but he waited for me. The day I turned sixteen, he gave me my first kiss. Then he was off to sea for six months. When he returned, I was waiting for him. He was seven years older, but I was so in love with him. He rescued me from the hellhole I called home. My only regret is that we left my little brother behind. He was already in trouble by then. I should have brought him with us."

"Where did you go?"

"We moved here, to San Francisco. We got out of that N'Awlins heat, and away from my mother, who drank herself to death a few years later. I was bored and lonely at first. Myles was gone for more than half the year. I was a baby in a cage until I went back to school. Then, I was in heaven. I was learning things, living on my own, in our own place. Myles would come back from each trip to a different person. He was with me when I went from girl to woman. He spoiled me rotten, but he also felt like he owned me. The more independent I got, the madder he would get, and that is when the temper started. But I swear to God he was trying so hard."

She broke down again. I really didn't know what to say.

After a few moments she regained her composure. I asked her what had happened on the night he died.

"I know you guys don't like me, but when you hear what I did, you are going to like me even less."

There was a terrible feeling in my core. Maybe I did have a soul because I really couldn't describe where it sat, but I felt terrible for deciding on her so absolutely. I knew that everyone had their own journey, their reasons for being who they were. Maybe it was the clash of tragedies past that had kept Sophie and Alice from being friends. Maybe there was too much of it in them both. I had taken a side instead of deciding for myself. My internal feminist was so mortified.

"I'm sorry I haven't taken the time to know you, Sophie," I said.

She didn't offer any apologies but exhaled as if to let it go.

"The night that Martha died, Myles didn't stay in the bar. He was cheap. He didn't want to buy a drink at the bar when we had liquor right here. So he came back here to pour a beer into the glass he took from the Jupiter. He did it all the time. He saw Martha look out. She did that whenever anyone came home. Like she was watching her flock. She was alive and well when he saw her."

"What time was that?" I asked.

"That was ten forty-five or somewhere around there. But when he was leaving, he ran into Dan. Dan told him he forgot his wallet. Myles told him to get a beer from the courtyard fridge, but Dan went into his place instead. Dan said that on his way back, he saw the door to Martha's place open, and when he went inside to check on her, she was dead already."

I was as surprised as I was confused. "Someone killed Martha between the time Myles left and the time Dan came out of the cottage? Why didn't Dan say anything to the police?"

"Myles said he saw her alive. I believe him. He would never lie to me. But once the police started asking questions, Dan told me what happened. I begged him not to tell the police. Begged him. He told me he wouldn't say a word. He said that Myles didn't seem flustered or sweaty or anything that would lead him to believe he had killed

Martha. He just had a beer in his hand and was proud of saving himself some money." She broke a little here but then regained her composure.

"Once it came out about Myles hitting me, and the choice Martha had given me, Dan was worried about lying. He started thinking Myles did it. I laid it on thick with him to shut him up. The more I stroked his ego, the less he talked about going to the police. I told Myles all about it. He was terrified and angry at the same time. It would look really bad if we went to the police, but he was willing. He didn't want me anywhere near Dan. I told him I would do anything to keep him from jail, and I meant it."

"Is that what you were fighting about that night? You were going to Dan, and Myles didn't want you to?"

"I didn't sleep with him. I despise him. I didn't always, but I do now. He has been enjoying the hell out of this control he has over us. Every time I saw him, he tried to talk me out of Myles. He just never got it."

"That guy gives me the creeps so badly. I really don't like him." I made a face.

My phone rang. It was Erik. I pressed "Ignore."

"I wish I could find my phone," she said. "I have people I need to call. Myles's mom is in Texas. It's going to kill her for sure."

"Is there anything I can do to help you, Sophie?"

She shook her head. "I need Elliot to get over here. I know he is having troubles, but I need him."

"You don't believe he had anything to do with Martha's murder?" I asked.

"Elliot? Please, the guy cries when cartoon animals die. There is no way he killed Martha."

I got up to leave. "I am so sorry, Sophie."

"Please, Lee, no one needs to know about what I told you. I don't want Myles getting blamed for Martha's murder. He didn't do it. Please don't repeat this to anybody."

"Okay," I said, not with any great strength of conviction.

It was dark, and the courtyard lights weren't on. I thought about what it was like here when I first arrived. Was it Elliot or Martha who always made sure the lights on the trees were on? I looked around for the outdoor switch and found it. The trees lit up to their former glory, but the spirit of the place had died along with its owner. I grabbed a beer from the fridge and sat to ring Erik back.

"Hey," I said.

"Hey," he replied. "Can you meet for a drink at the Jupiter?"

"Sure. How soon?"

"I'm here now."

I felt a sudden rush of heat and excitement.

"I'll be over in a minute." I left a note for Alice and walked over with my open beer.

Erik was sitting by the door when I came in.

"BYOB?" he asked.

"A little something I learned from Myles."

He looked at me for further explanation.

Jason greeted me without his usual cheeriness, which was only slightly more somber than a normally happy person.

"You okay?" I asked him.

"I'm getting tired of the tragedy, you know? Where's Alice?"

"She's still sleeping."

"Bourbon and soda?"

"Does a cat have an ass?" I replied, which was something I'd learned back east.

Jason looked at Erik and me. If he didn't like what he saw, we wouldn't know it. He was a great bartender, a keeper of secrets.

"So how was your day, Detective?"

"Why do people keep dropping in that little commune you're staying in?"

"I'd like to know the answer to that, but I don't want to step on any toes." I smiled and put my adorable plaid ballet slippers on the toes of his boat shoes.

We were looking into each other's eyes. The death and sadness of the past days were reminding me of how short life was. I felt reckless. My drink arrived and broke up some of the intensity. I turned back toward the bar and so did he.

"So…" he said.

"Sooo…" I replied. "What happened to Myles?"

"He drank too much; we know that. Then he died on a dock by the shipyards."

"What was he doing down there?"

"I don't know. He's a merchant marine. Maybe he felt at home there. He and Sophie had a fight. She went to her doctor; he went to the bar."

"But he had head trauma? Are you sure it wasn't a bruise from earlier? He had a fight with Dan in the alley the other day."

"Did he? What about?"

"Dan finally grew some balls and punched him for hitting Sophie."

"In the left temple?"

"No." I winced. "No, it was in the cheek. The left cheek if I remember correctly. I didn't notice a mark though. So he got hit in the temple?"

"Yes, hard enough to crack his skull and cause cerebral hemorrhaging. No one saw a fight, or at least no one is stepping forward to admit it. He could have run into some shady character. It's not exactly a stroll in the park down there, and from what I know, he was a bad drunk."

"It's so ironic that he died in the shipyards," I said.

"My suspects keep getting killed or injured."

"Do you still think he could have killed Martha?"

"He had some anger when it comes to women in power. But he was out of control. The murder was neat, and the killer was in command," he answered.

"Just tell me now, was it you? Tell me now, and I'll ask the DA to cut you a deal," I said, deadpan.

He smiled, which was like a laugh for most people.

"I like you so much, Lee," he said softly, like he was ashamed.

"I like you too, Erik." I really, really *liked* him. I was ashamed.

"It's too bad it's so complicated."

We both felt the sadness of those words.

"I've never been unfaithful to my husband," I confessed. "He had an affair with a coworker a year after my older son was born. We worked very hard to keep our family together. I couldn't screw that up now."

We were quiet, both of us holding our drinks on the bar, heads full of moral Ping-Pong.

The Jupiter was getting crowded. Before long, girls would be dancing on the bar. I was already feeling bodies pushing up against us, fighting for the attention of a bartender. Wally appeared from the back room to help.

"Let's get out of here," Erik said.

"Okay," I said, giving up every ounce of self-control.

He took me by the hand and led me outside. I was ready to go wherever he brought me. As soon as we hit the door, I heard my name.

"Lee!" It was Alice coming from the alley.

We dropped hands. My thoughts went from grateful to disappointed and then back again.

"Hey, sleepyhead," I said.

"Hey, Dummy. Where do you two think you're going?"

"The drunk crowd is in," I said. "It was time to get out of there."

"I need food. Let's go to LuLu's," she said, reading my guilty face.

"I should go," Erik said.

"Yes, you should, Detective. Don't you have a murderer to catch?" Alice said.

I was mortified and actually felt sad for him. Alice grabbed me like only a big sister would be allowed to and dragged me down the street away from him. My body started to cool as I got farther away. I looked back and saw him watch us go. *Wah!* I thought.

"Whore," my sister said as soon as we were out of range.

"Such a whore. Oh my gawd!" I replied.

"What the fuck are you thinking?"

"I am so not thinking. Just not," I said.

"It's a little late for revenge, Lee."

"It's not about that, I swear. Well, there is a small part of me that thinks I am entitled. I am just so attracted to him. Don't you remember what it's like to be married for such a long time? You don't feel like this anymore."

"It would destroy your family, Lee. Trust me. I speak from experience."

"I know that. I do. Thanks for rescuing me. I better get out of San Francisco fast. I need states between us…maybe continents."

Erik dominated my waking thoughts that night. I imagined a modern, noir-like apartment with light that came through the blinds. No dogs or kids or noise.

I fell asleep fast and had a weird dream about Hemingway. He was old and sad and fat. We were on a fishing boat in the San Francisco Bay. He kept trying to hit on me, but he grossed me out. I asked him to tell me about the Paris years, but his wife Mary didn't like it when he spoke of that topic, so he wouldn't. She was mixing drinks at a bar and talking to Martha, who waved at me. "You'll hit on me, but you can't talk about your first wife?" I asked. "It's different," Martha answered. "She knows it was true love, so she doesn't like him to mention her." Mary handed me a drink.

The sun shone proudly the next morning, holding my face gently as I woke. Alice had gone to work. Jason had reluctantly left on a long-planned three-day hiking trip with his college friends. I phoned home and brought myself back to reality. Then I made a rule. No more Erik and alcohol. The two definitely didn't mix. There was a plane ticket with my name on it leaving in two days.

Jason had left the teapot full of water and a loaded French press on the counter. I praised his godliness as the water boiled, then took my coffee out to the balcony. There was a dividing wall between Sophie's place and Alice's. Dan walked up the stairs toward Sophie's apartment. He hadn't noticed me, and I liked it that way. I sat perfectly still in the nook by the window.

He knocked on the door, but she didn't answer.

"Sophie, I know you're in there. Please open the door."

I could hear the door open.

"What are you doing here?" Dan said.

"What are *you* doing here?" Elliot scowled back. "She doesn't want to talk to you. And by the way, I know what you did, you little freak," he added. I heard the door slam.

Dan walked back down the stairs, still not noticing me. He threw something across the patio, and it went flying under one of the tables, then he left toward the alley. I heard the courtyard door slam.

What the...? I thought. I ran downstairs and grabbed it. It was a cell phone.

Why would he throw his cell phone away? I thought.

It was dead. *He killed it,* I thought.

"Oh my God! He killed it!" I said out loud.

I ran upstairs and called Erik. "Please get here now!" I said.

"Jeez. Good morning to you," he replied.

"No, really. Come over here now. What are you doing?"

"I just got to the office. I had a few after I left you last night. Drank away the thought of what could have been."

"I'm sorry about my sister. She basically raised me, and she thinks I'm one of her kids."

"She scares me a little."

"Have you met Lacy?" I laughed. "Anyway, you really need to get here. I think I know who the killer is."

CHAPTER 21

THE VULNERABILITY OF HAVING A large front window was not lost on me as I paced the floor of the apartment, too terrified to get in the shower. I got ready as fast as I could, applying mascara and some lip gloss. I was scared, but I also wanted to look good. A few yards away lived a violent killer, I was sure of it.

Elliot and Sophie left together, not even glancing into the apartment, preoccupied with grief and partnered in direness. I curled up on the couch, thinking I would be out of sight if someone came up the stairs. The door was bolted. There was a noise in the courtyard, and I took a quick peek and saw Dan. He was back and was looking around the ground for the phone. I moved to the door and watched through the peek hole. His search became frantic as he figured out it was gone. He went back into the cottage. I couldn't stand it any longer. I grabbed a sweatshirt and headed out to the alley. I was not staying in that murder factory a second longer. I swung the door open. Erik was standing there, and I screamed a little.

"Fuck!"

"And good morning, girl from New Jersey."

"Sorry. And I just live there. I'm from here," I reminded him. "I'm shaking. I'm so glad you're here. Look at my hands." I held them out as proof.

"What is going on?" He took my rattling hands in his.

"I know who the murderer is. Can you fix this?" I handed him the phone.

"What's wrong with it?"

"I think it's Sophie's phone. Dan had it. She must have left it in his house the night Myles died. He was bringing it back to her, and when she wouldn't answer, he threw it. I grabbed it from underneath one of the chairs."

"Please tell me what you're talking about."

"I have to tell you something that I promised not to tell. Let's get out of here."

His car was parked in the alley, and I practically leaped in. Once we were inside, I felt the panic fade a little and looked around.

"Jesus, is this the first time you've used it?" I asked him. His car was spotless. No cleat-shaped mud cakes or wrappers stuffed in the side pockets like mine.

He rolled his eyes.

"Just please pull away from here. I am so scared he's going to come out that door. Please. Go," I urged him.

"All right. All right." He pulled forward, and I could feel the relief.

"Shit! I have to go back there with Alice. You have to arrest him. I can't sleep there tonight."

"Jeez, Lee. What is going on?"

I filled him in on Dan's little game with Sophie and Myles.

"The guy's creepy," he said.

"That is exactly what I said. He is just weird. Who would want to force someone to be with them?"

"Someone sick," he replied.

"You should have seen him today. He thought he was going to be alone with her. When Elliot answered, he was pissed. I was sitting there on the patio, and I don't think he even saw me. But if he did, he might know I have the phone," I said, my voice escalating in panic.

"Well, you're not going back there."

"My sister lives there!" I reminded him. "And Jason's gone. You have to arrest him." I paused for a moment, and then said, "Let's go to a phone store and see if they can fix it."

"Good thinking, Detective." He smiled.

We pulled up to a storefront and asked the salesperson if he could help us. Erik flashed his badge like they do in the movies. I felt so official. The salesman was a kid and very excited to help.

He plugged it into a charger and said, "It's just dead. Look. Give it five minutes to charge." He excused himself to answer a customer's questions.

Erik and I looked at each other. We stood there, not saying a word. Again, the heat was traveling through my body to my fingertips. He wasn't letting up. The moment was intense and relentless, and I couldn't pull my eyes away from his. He moved toward me and touched my hand. It was just a touch, just a moment of his skin on mine.

"I'm in big trouble," I said.

"If you need to look at something on the phone, it's got a bar now. I'd leave it plugged in while you look though," said the kid behind the counter.

I took the phone, relieved by the interruption.

"Last call was from Myles," I said. "Ten thirty-six."

"You met me at the bar at ten thirty. I remember because I told myself I was only going to wait for you until ten thirty, and then you walked in."

"You knew I would be there?"

"I hoped you would be there." He was embarrassed.

I smiled. It was no accident that we ran into each other that night.

"Alice and I saw Sophie go back to the apartment before ten thirty, then. She told me yesterday she couldn't find her cell phone. Dan must have used returning it as an excuse to see her."

"You would think he would have deleted this?" he said.

"It was probably dead before he could," I said. "Poor Myles. He reached out to her before he died, and she didn't have the phone. But he could have called her at the apartment."

"If Dan told him she went home. Maybe he lied and said she was there sleeping."

"Did you look at Myles's phone?"

"We have it, but it's dead too."

"I will bet you money he didn't call the apartment. My guess is whatever Dan said to him was his last conversation with anyone."

"Just because he spoke to Myles doesn't make Dan a killer."

"He had opportunity. He was at the apartment alone the night Martha was killed."

"Why would he kill Martha?"

"It has to be him. Who else would find a body and not tell the police. He is so calculating, setting Myles up like that so he could move in on Sophie. He's a psychopath."

"If that were the case, you would all be dead. Why stop there?"

He had a point.

"I don't know, but he is the killer. I know he is."

"I can't arrest him because 'you know he is.'"

"No shit. We have to prove it."

He shook his head at my language. "You should have been a cop."

"Maybe I will be. I still haven't figured out what I want to be when I grow up."

"You'd fail the drug test," he reminded me.

"I'm supposed to meet Alice and Lacy for lunch. If they find out I'm with you, I'll never hear the end of it."

"Are you ashamed of me, Ms. Harding?"

"Ashamed of myself maybe."

We were quiet on the ride to the Financial District. He dropped me off a few blocks from Alice's office.

"Let me know what the phone says?"

"Can I see you later?"

"Alice gets home at six. We're making dinner at her place tonight." I shivered at the thought of going back there. "I can see you before then. Let's meet on the stands at three o'clock?"

I met Alice and Lacy for lunch as planned. I told them about the morning, including calling Erik. I felt completely justified in calling him. Alice rolled her eyes.

"What the hell was I supposed to do, Alice?"

"I didn't say anything."

"That freaky little worm," Lacy said. "That's blackmail. I could kick his ass."

I laughed. "You could, Lacy, no doubt."

"Seriously, I don't want you back at that house today, Lee," Lacy said.

"Trust me, I won't be anywhere near there today. I have some shopping to do, and then I'll hang out and read in the park until Alice gets home. Why don't we all meet at the Jupe at six and go in together?"

The plan was agreed upon, and they both went back to work. I went shopping in Union Square, and then took the cable car up Nob Hill and down to the water. I felt like such a tourist, but it really was the best way to get down there. I hopped off early and walked around the old neighborhood. The narrow streets were lined with tall narrow Victorians, painted in the colors found in a mixed bag of precious gems. There was the occasional midcentury apartment building, flat and modern, a "fuck you" to the painted ladies of the past. I didn't know anyone on the street anymore. Our house had been painted completely white. That was historically correct, but it still pissed me off. I wondered who slept in my old room.

My toes hurt from being pushed so deeply into my shoes as I walked down the steep hill. Erik caught my eye, and we smiled at each other involuntarily. A watching stranger would have thought it was new love.

"I kissed my first boyfriend on these stands," I said to Erik. "I grew up in that house right there." I pointed to the hill like he would know what I was talking about.

He was in no mood for my reminiscing.

"You were right about the phone, Lee. That was the last call Myles made."

I knew it, but hearing it made me so sad. Poor Myles and Sophie. It was inevitable that they would end in doom.

"I went to talk to Dan this afternoon. I didn't tell him I had the phone, but I did say that I suspected he spoke to Myles that night."

"What did he say?"

"He's a strange guy. I get a bad feeling about him. He told me some bullshit about how Sophie was fighting with Myles and needed a shoulder to cry on. He insinuated that they were in love."

"He's delusional!"

"I asked him if Sophie would back this story up, and he said, 'She may not feel it's appropriate at this time to expose our relationship.' And that he would like me 'to be sensitive to her needs.'"

"Nice try."

"The problem is we have no proof at all that he's done anything illegal."

"And why would he kill Martha? We still have no motive," I said.

I found myself feeling sorry for Myles. I kept thinking of him out on those docks and of Sophie with that creep, trying to protect Myles.

"Why was he on the docks in the first place? Sophie said he had no sentiments for the place, and she said she had never been there with him," Erik mused.

"Maybe he was meeting someone there?" I said.

"Someone like Dan. I thought of that. He says he didn't leave the apartment after Sophie left."

"Someone may have seen him leave. But the way he slithers in and out of there, maybe not," I said. "What's his apartment like?" I knew the answer but asked anyway.

"He's neat and very organized."

"It's him."

"Let's just say he's the best fit yet. They're running a background check at the station as we speak. I don't want you at the apartment alone, Lee. I don't have the manpower or the evidence to place another patrol there."

"If you're interviewing the residents, I'll be safe while you're there. I'm meeting my sisters at six at the bar, so we can go in together."

"Why don't you just stay in a hotel?"

"I would if Alice would go, but she won't. I know her. She has a baseball bat, and she knows how to use it." I smiled.

He drove me back to Alder, and we went in together.

"I promised Sophie I wouldn't say a word about the blackmail," I reminded him. "She doesn't trust women as it is. Let me go with you to explain, please."

The courtyard was as quiet and as creepy as when I had left it that morning. It was impossible to tell if Dan was in the cottage since it was still daylight. Sophie answered the door, appearing tired but calm. She invited us in, looking confused and a little out of it.

"Please excuse the mess," she said. "Can I get you anything?"

"No, thanks," Erik said. "I'm here to ask you a couple of questions about the night Myles died."

"Sure," Sophie answered, looking at me. She sat on the arm of the sofa with her bare feet on the couch. I thought about how I yelled at my kids for that.

She looked like a twelve-year-old sitting there—a lonely child of sorrow. I remembered being home alone after my mother died. The pain could still overwhelm me, even after all these years. I could feel my eyes welling, and I had to snap myself out.

"Is this your phone?" He handed it to her.

"Yes. Where did you find it?"

I told her the story from this morning.

"There's a call on it Sophie, from Myles on the night that he died."

She looked at the phone, which was dead again, and then started to cry. "Why are you telling me this?"

"I believe Dan answered the call," Erik added. "They had a fifty-six-second conversation."

She sat perfectly still, her mind working through the information.

"That little asshole answered my phone! Oh my God! The last person Myles talked to was that little freak!" She began to sob.

Erik gave her a minute to lose it, then said, "We know it was the last call Myles made from his phone. His death is considered suspicious due to the head injury. Have you ever known Dan to go down to the shipyards?"

"I have no idea what that little snake does with his free time," she replied. "Wait a minute! Do you think he did this to Myles? Do you think he could have killed him?"

"We're looking into it," he replied.

"It's no secret that Dan is in love with you, Sophie. I've watched him obsess over you since I arrived." I paused. "I'm really sorry to betray your trust, but I told the detective what you told me about the night of Martha's murder. He agrees with you—that Myles didn't hurt Martha, Sophie."

"If Myles saw Martha alive, then Dan was the last person to be alone with her before her death. He could be her killer," Erik added.

"But why would Dan kill Martha?" she asked.

"That is the big question, isn't it?" I said, looking at Erik.

"We're looking into this. So far this guy has been flying under the radar, but we're onto him now, and I am a little concerned about you being here. Do you have somewhere else you can go?" Erik asked her.

"I'll be taking Myles to Texas for burial once his body is released," she said, thinking out loud. "Elliot is staying at the Monaco. I can't stand being in this apartment right now anyway. I'll go stay with him until I leave."

"Thank you, Ms. Despre. I wish you would all get out of this place until this thing is settled." He looked at me when he said it.

"This was the first real home I ever had...and the first real family. It really hurts to lose it all so fast," she said.

I gave her a hug, and she patted my back awkwardly.

"Please call me at Alice's if you need anything, okay?" I said.

"Sure," she said.

I was nervous about being alone with Erik in my sister's apartment. There was way too much tension for sofas and beds to be in the same room with us. He got a call from the station before we got to the door.

"I have to go, and you are not going in there alone."

"Bossy."

"I mean it, Lee. Go somewhere else. I don't want you here alone."

"All right! I'll go to the Jupiter. It's almost time to meet my sisters. I'm going to need rehabilitating after this trip."

"I'll call you later. Be smart and stay away from Dan."

We were down the stairs and in the narrow walkway that led to the alley. Before we got to the door, he turned to me and we looked at each other for a moment. Then he put his hand around my neck and kissed me very slowly, not softly, but slowly. I was leaning against the brick wall, and his body was pressed tightly against mine. The incredible flash of heat and excitement that a first kiss brings was pulsing through every part of me. He pulled away, and I put my head against his chest for a minute. His body felt so good next to mine.

"What are we doing?" I whispered.

He faced me again, inhaling. I was breathing deeply and wanted him to kiss me again, but he let me go.

We walked to the corner silently, and I went into the bar by myself.

I was in a total daze. My internal conversation went from *What the hell am I doing?* to *I can't wait to do that again.* I was in big trouble. A kiss is cheating in my book. I was a cheater. It was official.

Cheater, I told myself over a drink poured by Wally.

"What's going on over in that hellhole?" Wally asked me.

I laughed. "Does this mean you and Diane aren't moving into Martha's place?"

"Hell no! I don't care about the free rent. I can pay my own rent. The bar's doing great, and I have some ideas to make it even better," he said with a new pride of ownership.

"Hey, Wally, did you see Dan out the night Myles died?"

He thought back. "Nope. I haven't seen that weirdo around in days."

I laughed again. "So you don't like Dan?"

"Never have. Aunt Martha didn't either."

"Why was he living there then?"

"It was a favor to John Boscoe. John worked here as a bartender for thirty years until he retired. He would have done anything for Harry and Martha. When he asked them for help finding his nephew a place, Martha didn't feel like she could turn him down. She said it was the first time she ever went against her gut feeling with a tenant."

"She had good instincts. The guy is so creepy."

"You ever see the way he looks at Sophie, all stalker-like?" he asked.

"Yeah, I've seen it." Then something occurred to me. "Hey, Wally, how did you find out Martha was evicting Sophie and Myles?"

"Martha told me, right here in the bar."

"Was anyone from the complex here when she told you?" I asked.

"No. No one. In fact, she swore me to secrecy..." There was a pause.

"What?"

"Nothing."

Something told me there was more.

CHAPTER 22

ERIK CALLED SEVERAL TIMES, AND I pressed "Ignore" and then finally turned the phone off. I was obviously distracted. Alice was watching me like I was a drug addict looking for a fix.

My sisters had met me in the bar that evening as planned. On the walk back to Alder, I filled them in on the day's events. There was an enormous sense of dread as Alice opened the door to the alley. The magic of this place had died. The ground was wet from the heavy fog. No one had turned on any lights, and there were no signs of life from any of the apartments except for the one I had left on in Alice's living room.

"Good, he's out," Alice said when she saw the dim lamp in Dan's window.

"Should we invite Sam to dinner?" I asked Alice. "I feel so sorry for him."

"I spoke to him today. He's okay—burying himself in work today. I think he'll forgive Elliot eventually, but he's not quite ready. Elliot is going to Texas tomorrow with Sophie. That will give them some space."

I turned the bolt lock after we came in.

"I've never felt like I had to use that lock. None of us lock our doors. We used to walk in and out of each other's apartments to borrow stuff all of the time. It's so sad," Alice said.

We made dinner together, quickly finishing the bottle of Tempranillo that Lacy had brought from home while we chopped and stirred a risotto recipe that Alice loved. Van Morrison's "Brown Eyed Girl" came on the radio.

"I can remember Dad singing this song to me," I said. It felt good to be in the presence of those who really understood what that meant.

Alice opened another bottle.

"So what is going on with you and the useless detective?" Lacy asked me.

They both waited for my response.

"Jeez, you guys!"

"Just spit it out," Lacy said.

"I like him," I admitted. "It's so stupid. I know! But it's so much fun to feel excited about someone. I haven't felt like this in so long."

"You're forgetting everything that comes with that feeling, Lee. You're forgetting the pain when it doesn't work out because he sees snot hanging out of your nose and stops liking you, or you figure out he's cheap or selfish and lose your feelings for him. It's always fun at first, remember?" Alice reminded me. "You and Jack have been through so much. He loves you the way you want to be loved. He's seen you give birth, for Christ's sake. You think the detective would love you after seeing that?"

"Think about spending the night at his house when you have the stomach flu," Lacy added.

"I haven't exactly had thoughts of dating him, if you know what I mean? More like a quick fling and a flight out of town."

"I'm the last person who should tell you what to do, Lee. But I speak from experience when I say that these little flingy things get you very high at first and hurt a lot later. You have so much to lose. Imagine how your kids would feel if they knew?"

"Oh God, Alice! That is so mean!" I said.

"It's reality, Lee. The reality that this very dangerous thing you are doing could bring your family down."

The thought of my boys knowing this about me made me cry. That, on top of everything else, was hitting me at once. I cried while my sisters made jokes, which made me laugh and cry even harder.

"What you need to do is get a life, Lee. Not a boyfriend," Lacy said.

"That's what Martha told me the day she died. Not the boyfriend part." I laughed, wiping the tears from my eyes. "She basically told me to stop bitching about living next door to the greatest city in the world and get busy. I'm paraphrasing, of course. But she was so right."

"What a great adventure you could have figuring it out," Lacy said.

Alice's phone rang.

"Hey, Wally. What's up? No, I heard from him earlier, why? Okay, well, I can have him call you when I hear from him. Lee? Yes, hold on." She looked curious and watched as I took the phone.

"Lee, I didn't tell you everything today. On the night of Aunt Martha's party, when we were all at the bar, I told Jason how happy I was about my aunt's decision to get them out. Sophie was being her usual bitch self to me, and I had been drinking pretty heavily. Any of them could have heard me."

"Was Dan at the bar that night?"

There was a pause. "Yeah, he was here."

"Thanks, Wally. You have no idea how much that helps."

I hung up and dialed Erik.

"Where have you been? I've been calling you for hours," he said.

"I'm sorry. I had the phone turned off. I'm with my sisters."

They were both watching me closely.

"I figured out a motive," I said.

"The guy is a nut job, Lee. I'm coming over now." He hung up.

I filled my sisters in on what Wally had shared with me.

"So you think Dan killed Martha because he found out she was evicting Sophie?" Lacy asked.

"I can't believe Jason didn't tell me!"

"Do you think Dan's at work?" I asked Alice.

"Where else would he go? I've never seen him with anyone else besides paid company."

"Do you think he leaves his door unlocked?"

"Are you insane? Who cares?" Lacy yelled.

The three glasses of wine were making me feel very brave.

"Who knows how long it's going to be before Erik can get a search warrant, or if he even can without any evidence. Let's go see what we can find in there."

"I'll go," Alice said proudly.

"No way. No way!" Lacy shook her head.

"Okay, you stay here by yourself," Alice dared her.

"Fine. Just what do you think you will find anyway?" she asked. "The police already searched his apartment."

"Yeah, but he had to expect that. He wouldn't expect it now. Give me a flashlight."

She handed me the light, and out the door we went, down the stairs, across the dark wet courtyard, and to the door of the cottage.

"Try it," Alice said.

"Should we knock first?" I gave it a little tap and no one answered. "Use your sleeves or the bottom of your shirt to open things. Don't leave any fingerprints," I reminded her. I was wearing a long-sleeved sweater and pulled the sleeve down around one hand.

"What were you going to do if he answered?" Alice asked, opening the door.

"Borrow sugar?" I suggested. "You go upstairs. I'll look around here. Take the flashlight," I whispered.

Alice went up the spiral staircase to the bedroom, which had an open rail from which I could look down. I started in the kitchen, opening every drawer and cabinet. Obviously he didn't cook much—most drawers were sparsely filled.

"He makes his bed," Alice whispered from upstairs. "He's very neat." I could hear her shuffling through paperwork.

"Eww!" I found his stash of porn in the TV stand, and let's just say he had nasty taste.

"There are girls' underpants up here. Sexy ones. I hope they're clean."

"Probably souvenirs from the hookers," I said.

I thought of the pot in our refrigerator and opened his. The produce drawer was empty except for a small baggy. I put my sleeve over my hand so I wouldn't leave fingerprints and picked it up.

"Holy shit!" I said. "Martha's necklace."

There it was. The necklace she had been wearing the day of her party—the day she died. I looked at it again against the light of the refrigerator. Small jade beads led to the pear-shaped green pendant, carved with lotus leaves and a frog and fruits.

"Did you hear that?"

The door to the alley opened. Someone was coming in.

I put the bag back and shut the refrigerator door so the light would go out.

"Please be Sam. Please be Sam," I whispered.

We both froze until we heard voices.

"Hey, Dan!" Lacy yelled from the balcony.

"Fuck!" I whispered. Lacy walked quietly down the stairs with the flashlight off.

We stood there watching from the window.

"Hey," he wasn't sure who she was and continued walking toward the cottage.

"Can you come up? I have something of yours," she said to him.

"Really? What?" he asked.

"My sister Lee found a phone in the courtyard yesterday. I think it's yours. Come up. I have it in the apartment."

He stopped in his tracks. "I didn't lose a phone."

"She saw you throw it, Dan," she said with authority. The challenge was on.

The two of them stood there, looking at each other for a moment. He headed up the stairs, and Alice and I looked at each other in horror. As soon as he went into the apartment, we fled the cottage. I closed the door quietly behind me, and we both ran up the stairs. It felt like I was running in water—I could not get to the door fast enough. And when we did get there, it was bolted closed.

We knocked, then banged frantically on the door.

"Lacy! Open up!"

I pressed my face against the window and saw him sock Lacy in the face. She swung back and ran into the bedroom.

Both of us were screaming and pounding on the industrial windows.

A moment later, she walked back down the hallway, calmly and alone, and opened the door.

"You assholes," she said.

"Are you okay? Oh my God! Are you okay?" Alice touched her face and hugged her.

"He's in the bedroom," she said and grabbed her glass of wine with one hand while Alice's bat hung from the other.

Dan was lying on the floor. There was blood around his ear.

"I told you I could kick his ass," she said, taking another sip, then downing the glass.

Alice and I both started laughing. Erik walked in.

"Hi, Erik," Lacy said and held her glass up to him, as if toasting. She looked like a wild woman. There had obviously been a struggle. Her shirt was ripped. Her right eye was beginning to swell. Her hair was pulled out of its neat bun, but there were still pins holding onto some of it.

Dan was coming to, but slowly. He held his head in pain.

"Well, Dan, you are in some trouble now," Erik said.

"Did you see what she did to me?" he moaned, trying to sit up. "She lured me in here and hit me." He touched his wound.

"I saw what you did to her, you little fuck!" I yelled.

Erik pushed me out of the bedroom and sat me on the couch.

"Please, please let me do my job now," he pleaded like I was a three-year-old throwing a tantrum. "Trust me, okay?"

"Okay." I believed in him, but I wanted to beat the crap out of that worm. He walked back to the bedroom and I followed, quietly this time.

"I can understand how you could be really angry about this, Dan. Is this how you were feeling about Myles when you met him down at the docks that night?" Erik asked.

"What are you talking about?"

"You were seen at the docks that night, Dan. I have a witness who is willing to identify you in a lineup."

He got up, hand still holding his head.

"He beat her! And she was going to stay with him! I had to get her out of that. She was afraid to leave. I did her a favor."

"By smashing his head in?"

"By getting rid of that loser."

"You found out she was getting evicted the night of Martha's death, didn't you?" I asked.

He was silent.

"I'll make a good witness, won't I, Detective?" Lacy asked.

"I think you will, Ms. Harding."

"I asked him if he killed Martha, and he told me he was going to kill me the same way. He said he would tie my hands behind my back, and then place a bag over my head, the same way he did that night. Then he told me some other really horrible details—really awful things. I think only the murderer could have known those things," said Lacy.

"What are you talking about? I never said that!" he screamed. You could see the rage. His pale face had turned red, and he was spitting when he yelled.

"Who do you think they are going to believe, Dan? Why would I lie about such disgusting details?" She was dead calm. "Am I right, Officer? Is that how Martha was murdered?"

I knew she was lying.

Erik didn't say a word.

"I should have hit you harder. If you were dead, we wouldn't even have to bother," she added.

"I should have killed you bitches in the park that night."

"I knew it! I told you guys, didn't I?" I felt so vindicated. "Why go all that way?" I asked him.

"All of this was Alice's fault. She's the one who went to Martha. She was going to take Sophie away from me. She needed to pay."

"So you thought I was Alice that night." I shivered at the thought of how close I had been to a murderer. "I told you he was a serial killer!" I said to them one more time. I loved being right.

Several cops arrived at the door a few minutes later. Dan was hauled out of the apartment in handcuffs. It was beautiful. They questioned us extensively, and we were asked to go to the station in the morning for formal statements. Lacy refused medical treatment and practically pushed them all out of the apartment.

Erik stayed behind for a few moments. I opened a beer for him, which he tried to decline but took without too much pushing.

"There are women's underwear in his bedroom dresser!" Alice told him. "That's not all. He has Martha's necklace. The one she wore the night of the party. He was keeping it as a trophy."

"And how would you know that?" Erik looked at Alice, who looked at me.

I told him the story of our home invasion. He did not look happy.

"We searched that apartment already. The panties were there, but that isn't so unusual. The necklace was not."

"Maybe he had produce in the drawer at that time." I tried to make him feel better about their failure to find the necklace.

"Do you realize you could have jeopardized the entire case if you were caught there?"

"He still doesn't know we were there," I reminded him.

He shook his head. "You are very lucky Lacy is as brave as she is." I got the chills thinking about it.

"And I don't need to remind you of the kind of danger you were in tonight." He looked at Lacy.

"I kicked his ass," she said again. Her glass was refilled, and she was determined to empty it.

A forensics team had arrived, and they were busy in the cottage. Sam had come home to more lights and sirens. It was getting old for everyone, but the effect it had had on his personal life were starting to show. The poor guy had aged like a president in the White House.

Detective Erik Healy went back to the station to do his job. I didn't walk him out, and we didn't say any private good-byes. Everything was done in the company of my sisters, who didn't leave my side.

Alice went down to the courtyard and turned on all the lights. We brought our wine and dinner down and ate on the lit patio. I knew from experience that the light fog would burn off and my last day in San Francisco would be a sunny one.

Lacy and I slept on the sofa bed that night. In the morning, we made coffee and sat on the balcony with a view of the cottage—yellow tape across the door. There was safety in being with my sisters. We would always look out for each other.

"Warrior women," I said.

"What, Dummy?" Alice replied.

"We are warrior women."

"Don't mess with the Harding girls," Alice said.

"We will fuck you up!"

"Lee, jeez! The mouth." Lacy laughed. "We have to get you out of New Jersey."

Almost getting killed hadn't gotten Alice or Lacy out of work. They left me, and I planned my last day in my city by the bay.

CHAPTER 23

LEAVING SAN FRANCISCO WAS ALWAYS emotional for me. I missed my husband and kids, my dogs, my bed, my life. This time was no exception. But every time I left, the sun was shining just a little brighter than when I got there. People were just a little kinder to me. The food tasted better than ever. The city shined white over the perfect bay, and the neighboring hills of Marin glowed green. The ideal sailboat floated by on the splendid glassy waters of home. I was a transplanted tree—a redwood tree. I wasn't thriving in the East.

Something was different this time. I was a visitor in that new town, and I couldn't seem to reconcile the old memories with the shiny new buildings and its chino-wearing residents. It was like the city I knew had died with Martha.

"I don't know where I belong anymore," I told my husband on the phone.

I walked out to the end of Municipal Pier for the perfect view of San Francisco, and then gave him the details so he would hurt too.

"We'll figure it out, hon," he promised.

But it had been eight years, so my faith was dimming. Each time I returned to the east, the hustle of life got in the way. New York City turned on its bright lights, and Thomas at Bemelmans poured the perfect martini, and I saw Diane Keaton walk down the street and no one harassed her, and I got to hear my favorite economist speak at Columbia for free, and I cried each and every time I laid eyes on Lady Liberty as I flew over New York Harbor, and Central Park cast its spell on me on a perfect spring day and I would think, "I will never get enough, see enough, live enough of New York." It wasn't an unhappy life. It was just as different as evergreens and maples—one stayed fresh and green year round; the other changed dramatically with the seasons.

I told Jack about the events of the previous day. He heard about the clues and snooping and drinking and the cops. I told him I had a crush on a detective. He was silent for a moment.

"Hey, as long as it parlays into more sex for me."

It was an old joke, first told when the entire neighborhood fell in love with a young contractor working on our house. I had told my husband how cute he was, and that was his answer. I liked his confidence and the freedom he gave me to admire the opposite sex. He didn't have the same privileges, for obvious reasons. I knew by the way he said it that he understood there was more. He was wise enough not to ask questions. I was wise enough to let it go at that simple, innocent confession.

After we hung up, I called Erik. It was time to say good-bye.

"Where do you want to go?" he asked.

"How much time do you have?"

"As much as you need."

He picked me up from Alder, and as I closed the door, I felt a rush of excitement in seeing him again. We headed down the coast, passed through the dense fog of Pacifica, and came out into the sunshine above the water on the steep cliffs of Devil's Slide. As soon as we curved to the bottom of the mountain and the road straightened, I told him to get ready to turn.

"Right there!" I pointed, and we turned onto a quiet lane lined with cypress trees and cottages. "There's supposed to be a ghost on this street," I told him.

"Do you believe in ghosts?" he asked.

"I don't believe in anything, remember?"

"Oh yeah. Godless Lee. I still have a hard time believing that."

"I did believe once," I said. "Veer left here. There it is."

The restaurant was a relic from the prohibition, built by bootleggers who smuggled their goods into the cove below. The back patio had unobstructed ocean views, sitting high on a bluff. The owners treated their customers to wool blankets, rocking chairs, and two big gas fireplaces facing the great Pacific waters. We sat on a bench and wrapped ourselves in plaid wool and each other. There was nothing to talk about. He wasn't going to ask me to stay, and I wasn't going to. We both knew that. He ran his hands through my hair, and I lived in the moment, without guilt or worry or sadness. We just were.

I told him about my parents, my wanderlust, and my depression. I wanted him to see the real me, so it didn't hurt. I don't know that it helped.

The ride back was quiet. He dropped me in the alley, and I asked him not to get out.

He held my face with one hand, so sweetly, and then leaned in. I took one last slow breath of him, and said good-bye.

A few minutes later I received a text.

"How am I going to make your face go away?"

EPILOGUE

◆ ◆ ◆

HEMINGWAY SAID, "I ONLY KNOW that what is moral is what you feel good after and what is immoral is what you feel bad after." His decision to leave his first wife must have made him feel bad for years. I was too tired to think about my own morality and even more tired of Hemingway. I bought an entertainment magazine at the airport and read it cover to cover on the plane. For those few quiet hours, other people's mistakes, fashion or otherwise, were like chocolate mousse for my soul.

I cried a little when I saw the Statue of Liberty from the plane window this time. Jack and the boys were waiting for me outside the security gate. I couldn't squeeze them enough. It was as cold as I remembered, cold enough to freeze tears. The ride from Newark to home was gray and depressing, like the setting of a *Mad Max* movie, all rust and iron. I stared out the window while we headed up a congested highway lined with big-box stores and malls until we turned off by the Porsche dealership and headed for the quiet streets of home. Life returned to normal—whatever that was.

"Life is about the journey, Lee. Isn't that beautiful? One long adventure full of skips and falls, dances and blunders, spins and

staggers. Embrace them! They make up our lives. The only ones we get to have."

I heard Martha's words often and was determined to direct my own journey. I was working on a new chapter in my life, one in which I could be happy in the present. The change I needed wasn't going to come from moving or changing loves—it was going to be driven by me. Once I realized I was in charge of my destiny, the snow melted and the sun warmed my face again.

Alder would never be the same again. Sophie moved out of her apartment almost as soon as she got back from Texas. She batted her eyelashes and scored a very cool place in North Beach. It was the first thing she did on her own. She had many lovers that first year and eventually set her sights on a partner in the firm where she worked. His first wife didn't stand a chance. I ran into her a few years later in Nantucket. She was the perfect second wife in her tiny white capris and navy-striped tank. Her daughter was the spitting image of her, all big-eyed in Lilly Pulitzer. The boy must have taken after the father, who was nowhere in sight. I had heard talk of him and some of his banking-money buddies starting a new yacht club—the New England establishment didn't like the lavish size of the new-money boats and homes and had denied them membership to the existing institution.

Alice and Jason thought about leaving Alder, but there were so many good memories—and they truly loved their place. They'd been saving for a bar of their own, and Martha's generosity had made the distance to their reality much closer. Martha's painting hung prominently in the apartment and eventually reminded them of her life instead of her death.

Sam's organization was growing rapidly, and a second branch was opened in Los Angeles. A year or so later, I read an article in the *Times* about his work. A twelve-year-old girl was growing a mustache and having a very difficult time with puberty. Her parents brought her to a pediatrician, where she confessed that she had always been in the wrong body. She was supposed to be a boy, she said. After some counseling, the parents took it well. The private school she attended did not. Resistant to the child's decision to transition to boyhood, they asked her to leave. The attorney for the family was Sam Larkin.

Sam and Elliot were able to repair their relationship. Elliot's betrayal cost them dearly, but they had a love for each other that mended the wounds. They interviewed many new tenants for the apartments and found some intriguing new residents...but that's for another tale.

The Jupiter continued to be a popular bar. Wally served up two-dollar tacos at happy hour and opened an outdoor patio in the back. Those in their midday youth still found an occasion to dance on the bar, but on some nights the Alder crowd could still be found seated at it. Diane got that house in Marin after all.

Dan went to prison for the murders of both Martha and Myles. It turned out that he had been the person of interest in a campus murder at the college he had attended. A female classmate complained to fellow students that she was uncomfortable with Dan's advances. Her boyfriend had confronted Dan and asked him to keep his distance. He was found dead a few days later. There wasn't any physical evidence to prosecute the young intern, but he was the main person of interest. The student had been bound and suffocated. And Dan was a well-known creep in the Newport Beach community he'd grown up in. He was accused of stalking a girl and suspected of strangling her cat when he was asked to leave the girl alone. Martha's instincts had been right. Her loyalty to her old friend had been repaid with death.

Jack and I returned to San Francisco for the trial. Lacy proved to be a powerful witness, and the prosecutor built a solid case. I saw Erik briefly at the courthouse. His new girlfriend was the assistant district attorney. She was a beautiful brunette with sexy shoes. We ran into them in the hall, which was slightly uncomfortable. The four of us chatted for several minutes before Alice reminded us we had a dinner reservation. I remembered his last words to me and secretly hoped he'd never forget them either.

The new Bay Bridge keeps inching closer to the island. I am designing my own destiny, as Martha advised, but I'm no longer sure that San Francisco is home.

The End

Acknowledgements

◆ ◆ ◆

Without the family of support I received while writing this book, it could never have happened.

My husband Glenn, thanks for always believing in me and supporting my dreams. You are the love of my life.

My boys, Jordan and Adrian, who have read their mother's words and been smart enough to discern between truth and fiction. Who tell me they are proud of me, which is food for my soul.

My mother, the most powerful woman in the world, taught me to be fearless. My father the adventurer taught me to dream.

Catherine Fernandez DeVos, I thank you for always telling me how great I am even, when you may not truly believe it.

Naomi Gamorra, I am so grateful for the many hours you have spent on my manuscripts, writing notes that make me laugh and help me say what I am trying to communicate in better ways.

Cassandra Longest, you are brilliant, and this book could not be without your keen eye and insight. You make me strive for better.

Edel Rodriguez, you are pure genius, and having your work on my cover fills me with honor and pride.

Jennifer ZacZek, thanks for making sure it all reads well.

Deborah Kaplan, my amazing friend, thank you for your generosity and talent.

The women at PDX Writers have supplied me with endless amounts of inspiration and encouragement. I am so thankful for the safety of their circle.

I'm lucky to have many great women in my life—women who understand how challenging and wonderful it is to be a stay at home mother, working mother, single mother or wife. We hold each other up with our powerful kindness and magical love. I am indebted for this lifetime to the sisters who have shaped me.

Made in the USA
Columbia, SC
26 January 2018